First Time Lesbians

3 Erotic Gender Swap Stories

Daniela R. Lovejoy

Copyright © 2020 Daniela R. Lovejoy
ISBN-13: 9798679459670
www.danielarlovejoy.com

Female Legacy

CHAPTER 1

"This can save my ass!" I cheered loud, jumping from one foot to the other on the wooden floor of my apartment as I waved the paper triumphant in the air over my head.

"What is it? Have you finally found a new job?" Sally asked, astonished over my scene.

"No, the letter is from an attorney. I've received an inheritance from my late uncle Gordon." Studying the note again.

"Does that mean you are stinking rich now, Alex?" She snickered sarcastically as she came over beside me and peeked at the paper.

"Don't be silly, Sally," I laughed "The rumor in the family was always that he had money, but he usually kept to himself living as a hermit. I think he was a professor in biology or something with molecules."

"The letter says you're his sole heir, so you must have known him?" She asked.

"Not really, only seen him a few times at family gatherings. The last occasion was a wedding three years ago, where we got seated together." I answered, trying to recall the moment from deep within my memory. "He looked scruffy, but we talked friendly, and he told me about some breakthrough discovery he was on the brink of creating after years of experimenting. It was all very vague and unclear since he wouldn't reveal more."

"Did you ever learn what happened?"

"That's the strange thing; no one ever saw him since he didn't show up for anything, some even wondered if he'd passed away.

"Clearly, you must have meant something to him when he put you in his will. This story makes me curious."

"It says I can come by at my convenience during their open hours. If you drive me there, you can tag along today and find out what it's about," I offered with a smirk.

"It's a deal! I first have a performance at ten o'clock tonight, so let's go right now!" She smiled excitedly at me.

I nodded. "OK, let's go!"

Sitting beside her in the modest green car on the way there, I thought to myself how fortunate this inheritance was. After I lost my job a couple of months ago at the factory, it had proved troublesome to find a new one. I didn't know where the rent money would come from, which was due soon. Sally, my 25-year-old neighbor, and good friend had offered to loan me some, but I'd declined. She worked as an exotic dancer at a local strip club.

I glanced at her while she focused on driving in the heavy traffic. Sally was a slender bombshell of a girl with long neon pink-colored hair, bright blue eyes, and an adorable face. She wore a short, tight tan blouse with a pink flower pattern and a rounded neck cut that was deep enough to show a bit of her stunning cleavage. She'd matched it with a pair of classic blue stretch jeans which hugged her curves so well they were like painted on her.

Sally had asked once if I wanted to see her perform, and that evening, seeing her naked had burned into my memory. Her body lacked nothing; it was slender with perfect big round breasts and a great ass that looked like sculpted on her. She was also so agile as she moved and rotated on the pole. She had the entire room, including myself, turned on hard, and she loved it.

She was a wild girl with an exhibitionist side and a warm personality. Anyone who got to know her just liked her immediately. My dick came alive in my jeans, seeing her in my mind, swinging around that pole again. I rested my hands casually on my crotch so she wouldn't notice.

She was perfect, and I was extremely attracted to her. Unfortunately, she was a lesbian, which meant we could only be friends. I envied the girls I had seen come together with her hand in hand and kissing her.

"Here we are, Alex," she said suddenly as she parked the car and brought me at once out of my futile daydream. We entered a fancy-looking building and were directed to a Mr. Williams' office after I showed the receptionist the letter. An older chubby gray-haired man greeted us with a serious but polite smile.

"Please have a seat," he said and gestured toward the two wooden chairs with leather padding placed in front of his mahogany desk.

"As the executor of your uncle Gordon's estate, I have been instructed to read the following for you from his will."

"For countless years, I worked on this, spent most of what I owned on it, but the reward was worth it. I believe you'll be a fitting heir to my legacy. It provides access to a new phenomenal world of unimaginable experiences if you dare."

Mr. Williams peeked up from the paper and opened a drawer in his desk. He handed over a small golden key to me, that didn't look like any standard one for a door.

"What is this for?"

"I was never told," he answered and shook his head. "I have to notify you that it's a limited estate, there's no property or funds besides a minor amount allocated to us for handling this matter."

"Is this small key all I inherit?" I complained in disappointment.

"Not quite. Are you aware of how your late uncle passed away?"

"No, he kept mostly to himself, and I don't think anyone has seen him the past few years." The face of Mr. Williams turned more serious as he wrinkled his forehead.

"About one year ago, he set up this will and informed us he'd travel for a while. He also stipulated that if we didn't hear from him within the next twelve months, we should consider him deceased and transfer his possessions to you." He leaned back in his chair with a slight grunt as he proceeded.

"This is a highly irregular manner to do things, so I can't say your uncle Gordon is regarded as passed away in the eyes of the law. That normally requires proof of death or sign of an accident, but we, of course, live up to his wishes and demands." He reached for the drawer again and handed over a more conventional-looking key to me.

"Before he left, he'd all his belongings moved to this storage space. You have until the end of the year to clear out anything you want to take possession of." He gave me a card with the address and number.

"If you would please sign this document to acknowledge that you accept the inheritance." He handed me his black pen with gold trim as I looked in disillusionment at Sally, this wasn't what I'd anticipated.

"What you got to lose, Alex?" she encouraged me.

I signed the paper and thanked Mr. Williams for his assistance and wandered back to the car with her. Inside, I was perplexed over the weirdness of this but also frustrated. I didn't expect loads of money, but I'd assumed there would be some to solve my rent problem and buy me more time to find a new job.

"Typical for my luck," I snapped as soon as we sat in her car. "When you hear about people who inherit a long-lost uncle, they always get money, and I needed that right now. Instead, I get odd words of legacy and some keys." I held them up in my palm and groaned.

"Yeah, bad luck, but don't forget the storage space; there might still be something decent of value which can help your situation and fit with that key." She suggested with a confident smile.

"You're right, want to join me on a treasure hunt? The place is close."

"Sure, but it's noon, so let's get a meal on the way, my treat. You can buy me a fancy dinner later if you strike it rich from what we find." She giggled while starting the car.

"Thanks, Sally." I smiled back at her. She always knew how to cheer me up.

We arrived at the storage buildings after a quick lunch at a nearby cafe. We parked near the gray metal roller gate marked 83 in high black numbers as specified on the card Mr. Williams had given me. I unlocked the padlock and pushed the noisy gate up. The place was crammed full. We squeezed in between the stacks of things, and began to search through the stuff. It was mostly furniture and cardboard boxes, a dusty, worn old green couch and chairs, a wooden coffee table with a loose leg, some kitchen chairs, and a table—all reasonably common and hugely out of fashion.

"Any luck?" I asked her hoping she'd found better items than me.

"Only some pots, pans, plates, and other kitchenware," she muttered while digging loudly through another box. I looked in others and saw only old clothes of his.

"That's odd," she suddenly stated. "Didn't you say he lived alone like a hermit?"

"Yes, why?" I came over to the box she'd opened.

"This one is full of women's clothing, and for someone about my age, I'd say from the looks of it." She held up a short pink skirt and a thong pantie. "It's about my size and looks new."

"No idea why he has that, but what's that shiny metal box underneath it," I asked and pulled it out and placed it on the coffee table. It looked exclusively made to hold expensive, delicate items. It was square and was about the size of a travel bag and was four-five inches high, with a locked lid.

"Guess this fits here," I said, holding up the tiny key and used it to unlock it. Inside laid something folded neatly together. I gripped hold of an edge; it seemed rubbery as I lifted it from the box.

"Eek that's an old blowup sex-doll," Sally screamed and burst into a loud laugh. I immediately let go, and it fell back into the container.

"Your uncle Gordon is a real prankster if that's his great legacy to you!"

She laughed so hard that the tears ran from her eyes and down over her cheeks while she leaned forward, supporting herself on her knees.

"That's not funny!" I hissed and slammed the box-lid.

"I know, I know, sorry it's just so ludicrous," She smiled at me and hugged me gently.

"I'd probably laugh too if I wasn't standing in the middle of it," I groaned. "Let's go home. There's obviously nothing of value here. Perhaps this unusual case can fetch a little cash, and if you want any of the women's clothes, you can bring that box along and check it out?"

"OK, thanks, some of the stuff looked pretty cool, and it was all clean and neatly folded." She added while we fitted the box of clothing into the back of her small car together with the metal case.

CHAPTER 2

I stood before the bathroom mirror after a shower and let my mind drift. Now my troubles persisted, and this day had started with such hope. I stared at my reflection with a huge sigh. 31 and unemployed... I looked drained and worn, my light brown hair needed a haircut, it wasn't short anymore.

Tomorrow morning, you take a tour around to the various construction sites in town and ask if they need someone for any kind of labor. I thought to myself. I was strong and wide-shouldered, so hopefully, someone needed some extra hands just until I found something more steady again.

When we got back from the storage space, Sally suggested we went out for a drink after her show tonight to lift my mood. I'd declined politely and told her that I was tired. The truth was, I honestly didn't want to see her sexy body move naked before my eyes. It would be torture when too long since I'd some actual sex.

I'd been so focused on finding a job, and I honestly didn't enjoy getting asked, "so where do you work?" when I tried to charm and score a hot girl in town. My ego was already bruised after losing my job, so my sex life had more or less been on hold lately.

As I wrapped a towel around me, a thought suddenly sprang to my mind.

Why had the old man kept that weird sex-doll in such a fine box? and the key so safely stored away with his will? Considering the storage place had contained nothing but worthless trash and clothes, some of it even women's clothes. What did he mean with those words?

This key gives access to a new phenomenal world of unimaginable experiences if you dare.

How could a sex-doll live up to such phrases? The man must have lost it in his old days. I suddenly realized that there maybe was something else concealed in the box and ran into the bedroom and opened it. I removed the doll and threw it aside while examining the case closer. It appeared empty; I searched the velvety lining of the inside with my fingertips for hidden items.

Nothing, there was absolutely nothing else in it.

"Cheap old asshole" I mumbled to myself, why make such a fuzz over an inheritance and importance of passing this on to me when there was nada. I looked at the shabby, rubber looking doll that laid wrinkled on my bedroom floor.

It seemed like a cast of a real person. The feet had toes, and the hands had fingers, fuck it even had dick and balls. There was a protrusion of a nose with nostrils holes and eye holes.

"Hmm," it couldn't hold much air with so many gaps, and was that a tiny zipper that ran along the front from the neck to the lower part of the stomach?

I grabbed it and held it up before me. It was about two-thirds the size of me, but in a rubbery, stretchy material, this wasn't a blowup doll. This was a full bodysuit made to wear, but why? It was in a faded orange-beige skin tone, but it was plain, with no markings or anything. If uncle thought there were unimaginable experiences in putting this on, he was kinkier than the average person.

I pulled the zipper. The interior had a sharp, shiny blue colored surface, which at first touch seemed wet and slippery, but there was no moisture on my fingers. On a further inspection, it was the material inside that just appeared that way. It smelled of rubber but also had a scent of flowers similar to freshly washed clothes. At least the old cuckoo had cleaned it after use.

I pondered, this was apparently the essential part of the heritage. Still not dressed after the shower and alone in my flat, I decided to try it on just once, and then I'd throw it out.

I sat down on my bed and stuck my legs into the bodysuit. The smooth inside made it straightforward to pull them through as I put my toes into the right little toe pockets and then stood and pulled it up. I fitted my dick and balls into the area for that; this was so unnatural. I put my arms into it and snug them through the arm-sleeves of it until the fingers were in place.

I stretched the outfit and took a deep breath before I quickly pulled the head part over my head and face and extended it, so my eyes, nose, and mouth fitted with the holes. I sucked in my tummy as much as I could and moved the small zipper gradually up until it reached the end.

I was completed enclosed in the bodysuit, which was an extremely snug fit, uncle was shorter than I was. I took a few steps across the floor, gazed down over myself. I looked the same as always just encased in a full rubber outfit from top to toe. I knew some folks had a fetish for this kind of thing, but it wasn't for me. I reflected as I shook my head and headed back toward my bed. It was way too tight and warm. I wanted to unzip it and get it off, but I became dizzy. It occurred swiftly and without warning. I collapsed onto the bed and passed out…

I woke up disoriented. The morning sunlight shone brightly in through the window.

What had happened last night? Why was I lying here so awkward? Then I remembered, the bodysuit must have been too warm. I sensed the tightness of wearing it.

I searched for the zipper, but my hand struck something that wasn't right. My eyes flew up as I gawked on my chest, which now had two sizeable protruding round bumps. They looked like breasts with nipples.

I sat up in a flash and stared down. I was still wearing the orange-beige colored bodysuit. This was undoubtedly boobs, and the curves and shapes of my body and limbs didn't look like my own anymore; they looked female.

I jumped off the bed and ran to the bedroom mirror while trying to get hold of the tiny zipper. I reached the mirror before my finger had found it. I gaped in shock. My reflection showed the body of a female with boobs, slender waistline, and a curvy hip and thin limbs. This must be me hallucinating from the suit I assumed. It was old and probably produced from a toxic substance that affected my mind.

I finally got hold of the zipper and forced it violent down in a state of panic. I pulled the bodysuit off, head and arms first, and then off my body when I removed it from my crotch I froze. My cock was gone; all I saw was hairless female skin folds between my legs. I rechecked the reflection.

Before me stood a pretty young woman with a scared expression on her face, she'd long wavy chestnut-colored hair. I moved my hand and tried to touch it and saw the girl in the mirror grab hold of it while I held the hair between my fingers. Was that me? I pulled my legs out of the suit and stood there naked in a mix of astonishment and shock.

She looked stunning, she'd a slender build with firm round breasts, big but not over-sized, each had a perfect slightly upward pointing pink nipple. Her arms were thin, with delicate hands with long fingernails. She had a flat stomach, with a narrow waist that curved out into a rounded hip that fitted with the size of the chest and gave her a softly curved hourglass shape. Between the legs, she'd smooth pussy lips. I turned to the side and saw a tight round ass that sat perfect, below it slender, graceful female legs, the skin was hairless and smooth looking.

I stepped a little closer and gazed at the face. The brown eyes looked like mine, but they seemed bigger on this smaller face with more noticeable cheekbones and a narrower jaw. The nose was cute, slightly upturned, and lips full and bright pink. She was shorter than I usually was. I noticed that the reflections I saw from my bedroom were different and viewed from a lower angle.

This girl looked younger, too, more like in the early twenties. This can't be happening; I slapped myself on the cheek.

"Auch!"

I cried with a female voice a lot higher-toned than mine had been. The pain was real and ruled out a hallucination. I was undoubtedly the girl I saw, but how?

My eyes caught the bodysuit on the floor. It had altered appearance to the shape of a female. The suit had caused it, that was what those words had meant, but then it could also change me back?

I clutched it and was about to step into it and pull it on when I spotted the broken zipper. Some teeth ripped off, leaving a long tear in the fabric.

"No, no!" I wailed. In the panic before I'd pulled it down so brutally that I'd ripped the suit and damaged the zipper. How was I going to use it to change back now?

I sat devastated on the edge of my bed and sighed, thoughts flew through my mind. Was I going to stay transformed into this girl shape permanently?

It was more than I could comprehend. As I leaned my head forward, my long hair dropped down over my face. I pushed it gently aside and gazed down over my body. The breasts heaved on my chest as I still breathed rapidly. They looked incredible, and I got an instant urge to feel them. As my hands moved over them, a new sensational pleasure streamed through me. They were firm but soft, too, and the skin so smooth. I caressed the nipples with my fingertips and let out a slight moan; they were so sensitive. I became aroused, and they turned hard from my touch as an unusual wetness occurred between my legs and needed my attention.

I pushed myself backward and laid down on the bed, staring up at the ceiling. Even though this body was new to me, filled with different senses and kind of arousal, my mind knew exactly what it craved most right now. I wanted to touch and caress my wet pussy, like a natural desire deep inside me. I rubbed my thighs together, but that wasn't enough.

"Ooh!" I moaned and squirmed on the bed, as my hand traveled over my flat stomach and onto the soft pussy lips. I caressed them with my fingertips. Electric waves of delight rushed through me from my crotch, and a warm sensation grew inside my lower stomach as I became wetter. The excitement was beyond words. My fingers became slippery covered in the warm juices emerging from my sex caused by my intense arousal. I rubbed my fingers over my dripping wet folds, spread them a little and let my finger touch my clit for the first time.

"Ooh, yes!" I moaned loud it was so intense and nothing I had felt before, so delicate but powerful nerves, so sensual good. With my fingers flat together, I rubbed my slick sex faster, caressed my slightly protruded clit while my other hand played with and fondled my breast. My back arched up, each touch was pure satisfaction, thrusting me toward the unstoppable climax.

I gasped for air, so much tension surged through every part of my being. Stroking the sensitive bud gently but rapidly with my fingertips made me cum in a series of repeated moans as pure pleasure shot through me while I became wet on my inner thighs.

I sank onto my back flat, sweaty and moist all over, still trembling from the strong after waves that passed through me while I tried to catch my breath.

CHAPTER 3

It took a while for me to regain strength enough to grasp what I just had experienced. Such compelling emotions and sensual enjoyment exceeded any masturbation I ever had done before. I curled up on the sheet and thought about how I could easily get addicted to this, biting my lower lip excited. At the same moment, it knocked on the door, and it brought me back to reality.

"Shit!" I squealed, that's Sally what am I going to do, she can't see me like this. It's also because I was so horny I lulled myself into forgetting how insane this whole situation was.

I got off the bed, shoved the bodysuit under it, grabbed the towel off the floor, and cleaned myself.

"Come in, I'm in the shower," I shouted with a hand over my mouth trying to sound as deep as possible, and close to my regular voice. I sprinted into the bathroom, closed the door, and turned on the water.

"Are you OK? You sound kinda unusual," she entered my apartment.

"Sure," I responded in a mumble, but I was I'm far from OK. What should I do my mind was in turmoil, I couldn't hide in here forever. The bodysuit was probably ruined beyond repair if it even could have reversed the effect. It was impossible to predict how long I'd stay in this form, so the best would be to tell Sally. Hopefully, she'd believe me and don't think I was some weirdo.

Even with the anxiety of having to reveal myself to her waiting outside, I almost got turned on again. Seeing how hot I looked in the mirror, but also sensing the fluffy cotton move over my skin, as I slipped into my bathrobe. It was several sizes too large for me now, but I couldn't think of anything else. I found a smaller towel to wrap around and hide my long hair. It had become chestnut-colored, this was all very strange.

I opened the door and stepped out; Sally was waiting on my couch. She was reading in a magazine and didn't notice me.

"Please don't get upset or leave, I got something..." I didn't come further before she interrupted.

"Sorry, I didn't realize Alex had company... wait, what you mean, don't get upset?

"It's me, Alex! That thing from the box wasn't a sex-doll but a freaky gender transformation device." I whimpered, knowing it sounded utterly ludicrous even to me.

"What?" She snapped. "Alex, you can come out now and introduce me to your friend. If this is a payback prank because I laughed at the storage space, I'm not falling for it!"

"There is only us here," I insisted and dragged out the bodysuit.

"Remember, it looked male, but it was something to wear, and when I tried it on, it made me pass out. When I woke up, both the suit and I had changed into a female form. I think I broke it, so I can't change back." I rambled while she stared thoroughly at both the outfit and me.

"Alex?"

"Yes, it's me!" I cried out on the verge of bursting into tears.

She came over and hugged me tenderly to comfort me. I noticed we were the same height now as I relaxed my head against hers. She laid her arms around me while she stroked me calmly over my back and soothed me. Her breasts pressed against mine through the robe. It was so good and instantly gave me a warm sensation inside.

I'm still so attracted to her even as a girl. I pressed my lips firmly together while pondered over my newfound discovery.

"So this was the invention… crazy!" she stated while I sighed. "So what will you do now," she let go of the hug and looked at me.

"If I'm stuck like this, I don't know what to do. I have nothing to wear. My plan to look for some construction site work is out of the window too." I answered, pessimistically sitting down on the couch.

"Alex!" she shouted. "If this is your uncle's doing, maybe the box with clothes we brought back was for you!" She dashed out the door before I could say anything. A moment later, she returned and planted the box on the floor in front of me. I'd removed the towel from my head, and the sight surprised her.

"You got long hair in a different color, too!" She stared and scrutinized my face.

"Yeah, it was a pretty thorough transformation," I responded as I got up and began to check the box.

"It suits you well. You look beautiful both your face and hair," she smiled and tilted her head. "May I see the rest?" She asked with a glimpse in her eyes.

"See me naked?" I responded, surprised, and stopped rummaging the contents of the box.

"You have seen me at the show, and seeing is believing, right?" She giggled. "Come on, don't be shy. I can probably better determine what clothes will fit you if I see your size and stature." At first, the thought was awkward; this body was so new to me still. Then again, I looked good, so I opened the robe and let it fall to the floor. Standing naked before her and moved a little to the side, which made my breasts jiggle slightly. She almost gaped as she saw me and stared up and down of me.

"Wow, you're fucking hot!" she chuckled with a smile. "At first, I wasn't sure what to expect from your story. Are the breasts and vagina real?"

"They felt like it" I smiled unsure of how to react as her enthusiastic praise made my cheeks warm.

"No need to feel embarrassed Alex, you look gorgeous." She winked at me and started to pull clothes out of the box.

"Thanks, Sally, and you too, it's just all very new, honestly a little shocked still."

"No wonder, here's a pantie and then try on this red cocktail dress, it should fit, you have the curves that will look ravishing in it." She handed me a lacy black pantie in a silky fabric and a short red sleeveless dress in a stretchy material. It was strange to put the pantie on, but it was so soft against my sex.

"Don't I need a bra too?" I asked while trying to comprehend which way to put on the dress.

"There's a bra here," she gave me the matching lacy black bra. "The straps will show on that thing, so you'll need a strapless silicone one, with this dress' low back cut too. Until we get you one of those, you can wear it without a bra which you can get away with easily since you obviously have firm tits," she giggled again.

"This all sounds complicated," I mumbled as I wiggled into the dress while struggling to control my long hair.

"You'll get the hang of it with my help," she reassured me while checking me out. "That dress is made for you. Now you just need some makeup."

"I checked in my bedroom mirror. I looked sexy in the crimson red little thing. It only had two narrow shoulder straps and a low chest cut that showed my natural cleavage.

"Aren't there some more regular clothes too? This looks more like something for a night out at a club or a hot date?"

"It mostly seems to be sexy things, but for my plan, you'll also need to look your best," she replied with a mischievous smile.

"What plan?"

"You said you still lacked money and a job, and the club has a vacancy for a new girl. Looking this hot, that spot is as good as yours." She explained while my eyes almost jumped out of my head.

"Are you kidding Sally, I was barely comfortable stripping naked for you and now you want me to do it in front of a room packed with horny men? Besides, I can't pole-dance." I retorted a little annoyed over her suggestion.

"It's nonetheless a solution to your money issues," she remarked. "Besides, you got over your shyness with me a moment ago, and you can dance and use a stool. I'll teach you a starter routine to use until you learn the more advanced stuff," she smiled sinfully. This was happening way too fast, first turned into a girl by uncle's invention and now next going to perform naked for strangers at a club. My mind was about to explode.

"Don't you want to work together with me?" She asked with a pouting mouth.

"You know I don't frown upon your line of work, and doing it with you would be great. I've just always been a more buttoned-up type."

"Check your reflection, honey. You aren't yourself anymore, but a sexy babe. You can continue to hunt for an alternative job; it was just an idea so you could earn some money." She leaned back on my couch. She'd a point, it was a solution despite bizarre in my mind, besides working the same place could be great. Her last relationship was even with a bisexual girl who previously had worked there, so perhaps this could lead to more.

The prospect made me a little moist in my crotch…

Fuck, I was a lesbian. I hadn't even thought of myself that way until now, Sally and I could become lovers and maybe girlfriends. Working a place where we saw each other naked would surely not lower my chances with her, and she'd called me hot and sexy. Perhaps she was attracted to me too.

"OK, I'm in," I said, hoping to myself it would lead to more than just a job.

CHAPTER 4

We met up in her apartment. I waited in her living room while she phoned her boss and told him she knew a girl for the vacancy. It turned out to be already tonight. I'd a time-slot at eleven o'clock if the owner approved me.

Sally planned a performance we could rehearse that would be easy enough for me to learn. For hours she trained with me, just us alone in underwear in the middle of her living room.

It was exhausting to memorize and do the dance movements but also exciting to be so intimate with Sally. When she guided my steps, we rubbed close together, and it was a constant turn on. I wished I could make a move on her and find out if she was interested too, but there was such limited time, and it was incredibly sweet of her to help me out.

Some of the time went with me getting the hang of the stilettos she'd lend me; we luckily had the same shoe size now. I already had some issues with my new lower center of gravity. Getting a pair of five-inch super-thin heels under my feet just made it worse, and then I not only had to walk but also move graceful and sexual alluring. By the end of the afternoon, I'd gotten enough practice, so I was confident I wouldn't trip on the stage.

"If you remember the various main steps of your program, that will help you keep track of the details in between." She assured me as we sat sweaty on the floor and emptied a bottle of water each.

"I hope I can, but if I can't, it's not your fault; you have been a good teacher," I said and smiled to her. She giggled warmly and gazed at me differently.

"Now I need a shower, so I'll head home," I got on my feet.

"You can take it here. There are clean towels in the closet next to the sink. Then we can relax and get something to eat before I do your makeup for tonight," she pointed toward the bathroom door out in the small hallway.

"OK, thanks," I replied and headed out there. It was identical to mine since the same building design though she'd a lot more products here. I only had soap, shampoo, shaving cream, aftershave, deodorant, and some toothpaste. Hers had several shelves full of all kinds of female articles. I practically gasped about what lay ahead of me being a girl from now on. Somehow it was also an appealing world. This transformation had altered something in my mindset and nature. My old self would never have agreed to this job or been interested in what good this facial cream did. I held up a small plastic jar. I guess I'll find out soon enough and put it back on the shelf while gazed at my reflection. I smiled, turning my head side to side with pursed lips. I was pretty, or hot I'd have said if referred to someone who looked like me. I took off my underwear and turned before the mirror.

I might as well enjoy this journey. The sexual experience I had so far was exceptional. I thought to myself and stepped into the shower cabin. The warm water poured down over my soft skin. I soaped myself in, letting my breasts bounce delightfully on my chest. I sighed quietly in enjoyment from the feeling, as I touched them and ran my fingers over my stomach, narrow waist, and down over my curvy hip. I closed my eyes to savor the moment shut out all outside distractions until I suddenly heard Sally's voice behind me and made a startled jump.

"Room for one more?" she asked, standing topless just outside with her head tilted to the side and a naughty smile on her face. Even in my imagination, I'd never pictured us together in the shower, but the possibility drove me wild inside.

"Always space for a sexy girl like you," I answered seductively, trying to play it cool. She smiled and pushed her panties down her thin legs revealing that shaved hairless pussy of hers and stepped in with me.

"So you are still into girls?" she whispered with a sparkle in her eyes, walking up so close our breasts touched.

"Very much so, especially you. If you knew how attracted to you, I have been for a long time." I replied as I touched her curvy hip with my hand and stared full of desire into her beautiful blue eyes.

"I have always known, you silly head, you think I hadn't noticed?" She giggled and shook her head."You were just the wrong sex for me, but not anymore, now you have become a stunningly sexy girl." She wrapped her arms around my neck and kissed me. I hugged her waist and drew her closer, her breasts and nipples squeezed firmly against my own as we both soaking wet started to kiss out of control. It aroused me and made me warm inside, her soft lips kissing mine.

"Mmm," I murmured as our tongues rubbed intimately, our bodies pressed against each other. My nipples turned rock hard from the stimulation. Her soft fingers and palms caressed softly over my sides. It filled my mind with new emotions streaming from my body; it was extraordinarily good. Her nipples had turned stiff too, and I became wet inside again. I gripped hold of her breast with my palm and squeezed the soft flesh gently. She moaned and kissed my neck. I bent my head back and closed my eyes, every little touch of hers sent waves of pleasure through me. The warm water splashed down over our bodies; it was unimaginable satisfying.

Suddenly she whispered, "Let's find out if your pussy is as real as you said, so you can understand how amazing being a girl with a girl is."

"Mmm, yes," I purred as she turned me around, so I faced the glass side of the shower cabin and leaned toward it with my palms. She pressed up against me from behind and laid one hand on my breast from below and groped it while she moved her other hand down over my stomach, approaching my sensitive folds. Her tits pressed against my back while she kissed my neck slowly.

I moaned delightedly from her touch as her fingers brushed over my silky wet lips, while also playfully touched my stiff nipple and licked my skin while I sensed her warm breath.

"Ooh, yes, yes!" I moaned as she rubbed my sex even more intense with her fingers; it was incredible. I was so stimulated and wet all over. She ran her fingertips over my hard nipple, and I'd to bite my lower lip in pure excitement and joy. These new erogenous zones were so sensitive, and when several were pleased at once, it was almost more than I could handle.

"Ooh, fuck!" I moaned out loud as I sank toward the wall pressing my breasts against the steamed-up glass side, as she spread my delicate lips and found my clit and gave it her fingers full attention. She caressed and enticed it with careful short steady brushes that made me gasp for air, and my heart was pounding wildly in my chest.

I moaned rapidly from each touch to the little bud, which sent immense waves of pleasure surging through every part of me. She nuzzled her face into my hair while her other palm brushed over my firm tummy and enhanced my arousal.

Suddenly something entered me; the feeling was unique but good and unexplainable to me. She was fingering me, and I almost screamed out my joy. I pushed my lower body against her hand, some instinct within me just wanted her to enter me deeper even though it was a first for me.

She fingered me faster, spurred on from both hearing and sensing how much I liked it as it drove me toward my climax. I rubbed my breasts up against the glass writhing against her palm and fingers inside me. I couldn't think clearly anymore, my vision blurred. I was totally caught in this moment of pure bliss as I experienced a long orgasm like nothing I ever had tried. It was more extreme than when I made myself cum earlier. This felt like a wet eruption inside me, and at the same time, energetically filled me with life.

I cried out several loud moans, which probably could be heard all over the entire floor of the building. My legs felt weak, and I slowly dropped to the corner of the shower base, shivering from the waves that still moved through me from the pressure released inside me.

She turned off the water a moment later and put a towel around me and sat down beside me with one of her own, and began to dry herself.

"That was beyond words," I panted scarcely able to speak. She smiled quietly with an affectionate twinkle in her eyes.

She looked so hot all naked and moist from the shower as she walked out to the sink and dried her hair. I got on my feet and dried too. Before she started to dress, I walked up beside her and laid an arm around her.

"I desire you and want to make you cum, too," I whispered in her ear and nuzzled my face gently into her lovely hair.

"Mmm," she purred and squinted her eyes sensual. I gripped her hand and pulled her into the bedroom and onto her bed. She was so stunningly sexy laying there all naked on her back. I crawled up and straddled her above her tummy, resting on my knees. I leaned down and kissed her soft lips, showered her with my desire.

Her nipples like mine had turned hard coming into the chilly room from the warm steamy bathroom. My fingers played them gently, sensing her reaction as she moaned faintly and closed her eyes. I groped her firm boobs with both hands and squeezed them carefully as I kissed my way down her neck toward her breasts as I pushed backward on the bed. I licked her nipples one at a time with my nimble wet tongue, tasted her soft, moist skin.

"Ooh more!" She pleaded while she ran her fingers through my hair. There wasn't anything I wanted more, kissing my way across her perfect tummy until I reached the edge of the bed and could spread her legs. I crawled up between them as she bent and leaned them out to the side.

I gazed first on her irresistible moist folds then turned my view to her face, letting our eyes meet in a glance. She looked excited, and I couldn't wait to lick and taste her as I crouched down and caressed her lips with my fingers first and spread them gently. Then I started to lick her pussy, pressed my tongue into her slit, and licked her clit with desire, let the tip twirl over it.

"Ooh, Ooh!" she moaned as she writhed. I sensed she became wetter, letting my entire tongue swirl all over her in rapid succession, licking up her juices. She moaned more continuously as she tightened up and arched her back, breathing heavy, which made her breasts heave nonstop on her chest. She was nearing her climax as she clawed her fingers into her bed-sheets. I wanted her to cum and added more tension to my licking, as my tongue tip flickered all over her.

She screamed out as I made her cum. She shook several times and moaned loud before she dropped back flat and laid breathing hard. I crawled up beside her while I licked the last bit of her wetness of my lips.

She smiled exhausted as I cuddled next to her filled with delight as I thought about our time in the shower and now here. It was the best sexual experience ever. I loved to be a girl with super sensitive nerves that made sex so incredibly more intense and better. Mostly I loved to be together with Sally finally. I grinned wide, thinking of how many other experiences like this awaited me.

I didn't care anymore if I couldn't turn back into my old self. It wouldn't surprise me if uncle Gordon had come to the same conclusion and lived his life as a girl somewhere. In fact, I was confident he was still alive, knowing what I knew now the pieces fitted together. He'd waved his old life goodbye and passed his legacy on to me for some reason, his female legacy.

"You look far away, what are you thinking about?" she asked softly, looking sweetly at me.

"That I'm happy, being like this right here with you."

"I'm glad to hear, I feel the same way," she said and leaned over and kissed me gently. "Wish we could lie and cuddle some more, but now I need another bath, and we need to get you ready for tonight."

"Oh, crap! I'd utterly forgotten!"My world had been confined only to be Sally and me naked together. All other things had vanished into oblivion.

CHAPTER 5

Two hours later, we were sitting in her car, heading to the club, and my new job. I was back in the tight, revealing red dress still braless, and her black stilettos. She'd also lent me a dark coat until I could get some clothes of my own.

Sally had said it was important I was as sexy as possible to impress when I met her boss. He only wanted employees that looked hot. She'd told that even though he seemed rough and overly fond of watching naked women, he was honest and made no approaches toward the girls working for him.

Part of me was nervous and wished I didn't have to do this, but another part was excited and looked forward to doing it. Perhaps a lingering last part of my old self struggled within me with my new.

We parked at the back and entered through a personnel entrance where one of the staff greeted her and let us inside.

I'd never seen this area of the club which appeared old and less maintained, compared to the public space which had looked fancier when I visited to see her perform. It had dimmed reddish light, a large modern bar section, and rows of small wooden tables with chairs along the stage, which was narrow but reached far out into the middle of the floor.

"So you're the girl who wants to work here?" The voice sounded monotonous and came from a short, stocky, almost bald man with a flat face in a cheap-looking suit who examined me thoroughly with a horny stare.

"Yeah, my name is Alex," I answered with a sweet voice. I threw my hair to the side with a quick turn of my head while I swayed my hip and rested my palm on it, trying to look appealing and sexy. I was, for the first time, happy Alex was a common girl's name too. It had always bothered me enormously.

"OK, I'm Owen Miller, and this is my club, you'll have one trial tonight and only get the job if you live up to the expectations." He made a narrow smile and seemed to look forward to inspecting a new girl as he went out to the public area.

"Don't worry, just go get ready and do as I taught you. I'll tell the DJ to use the music we used back at my place." Sally said reassuringly while hugging me.

"I have also found a fitting stage name for you," she whispered, "it's Destiny." She smiled and directed me toward the tiny wardrobe where I could change into the show bikini she'd given me as a starter gift.

There was a huge-breasted girl there busy with her makeup, I nodded, and we exchanged a friendly "Hi." I got out of my clothes and put on the black g-string and a small triangle top with a simple lock on the back for easy removal. The top and bottom were polyesters with gold flakes woven in the fabric that sparkled in the light.

I checked myself quickly in the wardrobe mirror. The skimpy outfit contrasted nicely against my pale skin and left almost nothing to the imagination. That was, of course, also the whole point of the show. Sally had laid a heavy makeup which close-up seemed too much. She'd told it looked great for the crowd seeing it from a distance. The room was cold and made my nipples turn hard and visible through the top.

I stood outside the stage, nervous in darkness, and as they announced. "Next, here comes Destiny!" The music started, and the deep heavy beat pounded through the entire building as I with springs in my steps entered and gripped hold of the chair.

I wiggled my entire body, let my breasts shake, and tossed my hair from side to side. Then slung a leg over the chair, strutted to the rhythm of the tune out to the edge of the stage and back again, toward the chair with a hip swing in every step. I was letting all get a sense of my slender legs that looked super long in these five-inch heels and behold my firm round ass jiggle mesmerizing on the way back.

The spotlights were sharp and turned the entire room almost pitch black from my point of view. From the shadows, it appeared half full of people tonight. I spotted Sally off to the side near a place where a bit of the stage light lit up her face enough so I could see her follow me intensely. Someone made a wolf whistle, and it spurred me on. The beat got in my blood; I was going to show them what I could.

I ran my hands over my body and danced seductively around the chair several times. I put one leg on the seat, again moving my fingers over my breasts and body, down over my legs, before straddling the seat reversed with my back facing out to the crowd. I twisted my legs around the back of the chair and bent over backward so that my upper body and head faced toward the audience upside down.

This thin body was so nimble and agile; I felt light as a feather. I ripped my top off and let my boobs hang free. The gravity pulled them toward my head. Then I leaned up again and turned 180 degrees, moving one leg over the chair backrest, so I faced out toward the crowd. I heard multiple cheers while spreading my legs and ran my hands over them, letting my naked breasts bounce as I shook my upper torso to the music swaying side to side.

Then I strolled back and forth across the stage a few more times flexing my body, pushing my boobs together and squeezing them, letting them swing and bounce. I turned and moved my hips from side to side, shaking my ass before sitting on the chair again. I spread my legs and leaned forward, letting my fingers run up over them from my feet until I reached my crotch, where I brushed my fingertips over the pantie with open mouth and closed eyes. My neck and head leaned back, looking aroused.

I pressed my legs firmly together, and with a few fingers on each hand pushed my thin pantie off my legs, now I was all nude. I quickly spread my legs just for a moment before pressed them together again, as I turned ninety degrees on the seat and arched backward. My legs stretched out long to the other side to entice the audience who knew I was all naked, as I moved my hands down the sides of my body.

I got a short glimpse of Sally; she cheered for me. I spun to face the front again, spreading my legs and squeezed both my breasts. Then I got up and walked out to the end of the stage as the music was nearing its end. I turned, letting my back face the crowd. I spread my legs and leaned, revealing forward, touching my feet with a sliding movement of my hands before I walked back and stopped beside the chair. Put a leg on it and froze as the music stopped, and the main spotlights switched off.

The whole club cheered and whistled while I was completely out of breath. I grabbed my clothing pieces from the floor next to the chair and got off the stage. I hurried into my own pantie and dress just in time before Owen showed up with a grin on his face.

"Impressive performance. Sally said you were fairly new but talented, and she was right." His eyes glanced over me and then turned to my face again. "You're hired! Come by the club tomorrow afternoon; then we'll get the paperwork setup."

"That's great, thank you, Mr. Miller." I was so relieved it had paid off and not been for nothing, solving my money problems. I was high on adrenaline, still from the excitement of the show, and the anxiousness, I'd been filled with before the start.

Sally came out to me, beaming with pride and happiness. "I hear you got the job. Congratulations! You made me so proud. I knew you had it in you!"

"Very much thanks to you," I smiled.

"You did really well, especially for your first time." She giggled as I grabbed the coat and we headed out to her car.

"Many things have been the first time today; it's been an extraordinary day." I gripped her hand and gazed into her beautiful eyes.

"This may come rather soon and out of the blue, but I love you Sally and everything about you." It was my true feelings, but I wanted to bite my lip as I heard the words leave my mouth and saw she stared at me silently. My head was spinning after this day. It was too quick to spring such a declaration of love on her in a back parking lot on a dark, cold evening. I should have given her more time to get to know my transformed self. I got angry at myself for not waiting as she spoke.

"I love you too, Alex," she replied and leaned close and kissed my lips warm and sweet. I could barely keep my feet on the ground as we got into her car. She started the engine and said with a giggle and a quick wink at me.

"Maybe you end up not even needing this money for rent," I laughed and replied. "Maybe we can use some of them on clothes. I need some casual too."

"Else, I wouldn't mind seeing you wear that revealing dress every day, but you are right; it also needs to be washed and what to do then?" She laughed as she reversed the car out of the space.

"That day we could spend in bed together naked," I replied, making us both laugh.

"You're just as naughty minded as I am." She giggled as we headed home, ending a day that turned out to be the best day of my life. I'd a feeling the coming days, weeks, and months might become even better.

My Lesbian College Love

CHAPTER 1

"Do you love me?"

"She asked you that out of nowhere?" My friend nodded, taking another swig of his beer.

"What did you say to her? You two have been together, inseparable almost, for the past month."

"I didn't know what to say to her. I ended up looking like a dumb, mute animal. How can she just ask 'Do you love me?'"

"I bet she didn't take such a lack of response well."

"No, not at all! She surprised me, I thought we were having mutual fun... you know, no strings. That's what she said when we met." He took another sip of beer. "A shame though, she's such a wild girl in bed, she even..."

"Yes, thank you! I don't need to hear more about your sleazy adventures on the sheets. I have heard enough of your frequently, sexual exploits the past weeks."

"That's because it's too long since you had a girl yourself... Have there been any, at all, since Linda?"

"Not really…" I replied, irritated. He hit a tender spot. A few months back, Linda and I were quite a pair. We joked and laughed together, shared many interests, and our sex was good… no, it was great! She was a stunning girl who took her fitness seriously. I train too, a couple of days each week, at the gym. In all modesty, I'm a good-looking guy. All said we fit perfectly together, though it turned out she didn't reciprocate my affection for her to the same degree. That, I first learned an evening where she, to my utter surprise, dumped me for the star quarterback. It was a blow I didn't see coming. It knocked the wind out of me. Mike's reminder made me think about how his latest fling was feeling right now. Probably about the same as I did that evening. I wished the breakup hadn't hit me so badly, but with my heart so involved, I couldn't discard it as easily as a candy wrapper. I'd needed the time to let it settle.

"Stop sulking about her, Tom. We're both single, and this place is one huge hunting ground for girls. Why do you think I asked you to come along for this frat party?" He said, surely seeing his talk of Linda had made my gaze empty and sad.

"I know, but we're sophomores now. We can't just let it be parties and girls, like when we were freshmen. I need to start focusing more on my grades, and I have an advanced math test tomorrow. I can't even imagine why they throw this party on a school night instead of the weekend."

"Because they, just like yours truly, know that nothing should stop a good party." He waggled his eyebrows at me and emptied his beer.

"I'll call you when I find a couple of sexy girls for us."

He left, with his always larger-than-life confidence, into the steamed up room filled with young people dancing to the loud eternal beat, that hammered out through the speakers.

Mike was my best friend here at college. We met when we became roommates in the first semester. We shared a small two-person dorm room in a three-story building at the campus area. We had great fun together, even though we were different in several ways. He was the more extrovert of us, thus dragging me out to this party tonight. Else I had probably stayed at home, preparing one more time for tomorrow's test.

I wondered if he ever would take his studies seriously. I wanted something out of my time here; secure my future. Though, I also envied his carefree way of seeing things. Everyone said that college should be the best time of my life. For a while, it was just too short. I emptied my beer. The equation rules of my impending test crept into my mind strong enough to push the music into the background.

Suddenly my eyes caught a girl with long straight auburn colored hair standing at a nearby table, decked with a large punch bowl and snacks. She chatted with three other girls, holding a glass of punch. I'd never seen her before, beautiful blue eyes and some cute dimples, which appeared by the corner of her mouth when she smiled. Her lips looked so inviting; moving mesmerizing while she talked and laughed.

On this mild fall evening, she wore a white super tight strapless crop top. It looked so hot on her and showed off her slender tummy too. She matched it with a pair of classic blue denim shorts, which highlighted her lovely tanned legs.

Everything but her vanished from my mind, I needed to talk to her, so I walked over beside them.

"Is the punch any good?"

"It's okay," a blonde girl beside her replied. Another just shrugged her shoulders.

"Someone added way too much rum instead of vodka to the mix." The auburn beauty spoke with a velvety soft voice. She frowned a little and wrinkled her nose, looking so incredibly cute doing so.

"Then I'll skip the punch, care to dance?"

"No, thanks." She replied fast but polite.

"Perhaps after you have finished your cup of rummy punch?"

"Really not interested." She smiled, but her facial expression left me no hope of changing her mind. I headed back to the other table and found another beer, but never got around to open it. I thought like crazy on something to say to this super hot girl that wouldn't sound corny; something that would let me have at least her name. I was struck hard by her beauty. She illuminated the room, blinded out every other person, the heat of the crowded space, the smell of spilled beer, and the loud music.

"You are hit bad," a sharp female voice said next to me.

I turned my head. A girl not looking older than my 19 years, leaned up against the table, almost rubbing elbows with me.

Her appearance was strange. She looked like a clash between a goth and a hippie. Mixing heavy dark makeup, rivets covered black boots, choker, and bracelets, with a loose fit dark red-colored flowery top and skirt. She was standing out from the average crowd, but her weird attire couldn't hide that she was an attractive looking girl.

"What you mean?"

"You have lost your heart to a girl you don't even know," she retorted, looking not at me but toward her.

"Do you know her?

"Maybe I do, maybe I don't."

"That's not a helpful answer to my question, and I'm really not up for riddles."

She suddenly moved closer, rubbing her thigh against mine as she turned her head. Her amber-colored eyes stared into mine up close, making me for a moment believe that she's going to kiss me, with those dark, lush lips of hers, but then she, with an alluring whisper, said.

"The real question is: Are you willing to do all that's needed to have a chance of, her becoming yours, and you becoming hers, no matter what?"

"Sure…?" Her question was odd, and my reply far from confident.

She reached down into a sewn-on pocket, sitting on the right side of her skirt, and picked up something. She gripped my hand and pressed it hard into the palm. When she let go, I looked down at a small dark red polished stone heart.

"What am I supposed to do with this? Is it something to give her?"

"No! Before you go to bed tonight, hold the heart firmly inside your palm, and think of her as strongly as you can. Then keep it close to yourself while your sleep."

"Is that your help?" It flew out of me loud after hearing her nonsense. I turned my eyes away from the little heart, looking toward my dream girl again, just to discover that the small group had left while talking with the stranger beside me. I looked toward her, still waiting for an answer, but she was gone too. I spun around looking, but she was nowhere to be seen.

What a weirdo. Honestly, I was more concerned about the whereabouts of the gorgeous girl with the auburn hair. I spend the next 30 minutes looking for her. A bottle, aimed for my head, missed it by a few inches as I walked in on a couple, already busy in one of the rooms. But looking everywhere, my search still came out empty. It seemed she had left early, and no one knew her based on my description.

Scanning all over the fraternity house, I hadn't seen Mike either. He's probably already making out with a new girl somewhere and forgotten all about me; I pondered to myself. It wouldn't be a first when he got a girl on his radar.

I decided to head back to campus and our dorm room. I took a deep breath of cool fresh air as I left the house. I kicked a beer can off the front lawn, as hard as I could. Now that goth hippie had cost me my chance of talking more with her. That limited my possibility of ever meeting her again. The campus was huge, and I couldn't even be sure she was a student there and not just here tonight with a friend. I stuck my hands into my pockets, inhaled another breath of cold evening air, and walked home.

CHAPTER 2

To my relief, I found our room empty. I just wanted to crawl to bed and sleep after this disappointing evening, and with the impending math test early tomorrow. I finished up in the bathroom in a hurry. Our room had it's own small one, thanks to the building being fairly new.

I moved through an obstacle course of Mike's mess to get to the bed and my side of the room. His clothes and sports equipment were lying all over the floor. A few soda cans lay scattered around the trashcan in the corner, from his missed 3 point shots. I needed to talk with him again tomorrow about keeping this place a minimum of cleaned up. Even for a boy's dorm room, this was too much. As I laid my jeans on the chair at the end of my bed, the small heart fell out of the pocket and tumbled over the wooden floor, until his basketball stopped it.

I guess some positive thoughts can't hurt. I picked up the little heart and slipped under the covers. I held it firmly inside my palm, seeing her dimpled smile and great body again in my mind. Then I reached up and put the stone next to my phone at the end of the dresser, standing next to my bed. I closed my eyes; let the tiredness push away any thoughts, so the sleep could take over.

"Open your books on page 248." Our lecturer, Mr. Hall, called out in math class. Why am I the only one here? I looked around at all the empty rows. I turned to face Mr. Hall again. Instead of seeing him stood a sexy girl with long wavy black hair by the blackboards. She wore a short light orange sleeveless dress. It hugged her body, showing off her slender, curvy frame and the smooth tanned skin of her long legs. Her face showed delicate features, big brown eyes, a button nose, and lush lips. She looked toward me, smiling welcoming with a gleam in her eyes. The gray walls surrounding us vanished, and a clear blue sky became her backdrop. A refreshing breeze kissed my face, carrying a warm scent of intoxicating apple and vanilla.

She, almost in a dance, turned around, letting the sun be her personal spotlight. I gawked as she pushed the thin straps over her shoulders. The dress slid down and off, revealing her goddess-like body to my hungry eyes. A pair of teardrop-shaped breasts bounced firmly on her chest. The cool air made her upward-facing pink nipples stiffen.

Her other hand's fingers moved down over the naked, smooth skin of her body; over her narrow waist and slender stomach. She let a fingertip brush past her vertically shaped bellybutton, turning my attention onto her naked shaved folds. She waved me teasingly closer while stepping backward. As I moved toward her, she laughed, but I heard no sound. She then turned around and started to run away in a light jog… Now viewing her from behind, she showed off her round, tight buttocks.

I didn't know who this hot girl was and why she wanted me to follow her, but I needed to comply with her commands, like I was under her spell. I caught up with her at a small idyllic cottage. Large thick green trees surrounded it. The ground covered with scented flowers in every color of the rainbow. She opened the door, took my hand, and led me inside. As she closed it, I stood in a cozy room. It was lit up by dozens of candles. They let a playful, warm light caress every bit of her sexy body. I kissed her cherry lips, so soft, and delicious while the vanilla apple scent of her hair nurtured my nostrils, making me want to inhale her deep.

She gripped my wrist and pushed my hand against her breast. So firm but soft skin, such a sensual handful to fondle, she purred satisfied from my fingers caressing the flesh, touching her stiff nipple while savoring the moment of her lips against mine. My tongue found hers, twisting in a wet kiss of desire.

"Mmm," she moaned as I squeezed her boob and flicked a couple of fingers smoothly over her nipple. She grabbed my other hand, pushed it down against her crotch. I felt her silky smooth folds under my fingers. Warm, soft, and moist; all at the same time; a potpourri of feelings moving through my fingertips and into my mind. She held her hand firmly against mine. If she wanted me to please her, I obeyed this naked goddess's wishes with the greatest of pleasure. I caressed her lips, moving my entire hand back and forth between her legs. I pressed a finger between the folds and found her button clit. I circled it with my fingertip, making her grind her pussy against my hand while I cupped her breast with my free hand. I added another finger, rubbing her now coaxed clit soft but steady up and down as her juices wet my fingers, pressed against her steaming hot sex.

I couldn't resist the temptation any longer and moved two fingers down to her tight, wet entrance, and bent them into her. She shivered against me as I pressed them slowly into her soaking depths, moving them in and almost out, in a constant move. Her juices flowed over my fingers. I squeezed her breast brief and sudden, making her moan louder and love-bite my lower lip. She rode my fingers hard, now buried as deep as possible inside her.

She clenched around them, as I made her cum. She broke free of our kiss, tossed her head backward in a loud moan while clinging to me with both her arms. I felt her girl cum wet my hand even more. For the first time, I noticed a red stone heart hanging around her neck in a short necklace; I hadn't seen that before now.

My vision blurred completely, and suddenly I shivered heavily being so warm and… wet? I regained my sight and stood opposite myself? I stared at the person in front of me; it was me. I saw the arms reaching over toward my position touching me. I looked down; the hands touched… one of my naked breasts and my crotch, I felt the fingers deep inside me!

My eyelids flew open as I rushed up sitting, feeling sweaty all over, panting while my heart pounded in my chest.

Shit…! What a hot and sexy dream, with a surreal end… I couldn't recall ever seeing that black-haired girl before. I tried to salvage the images before they vanished like water in hot sand. But they faded away, became unclear like dreams so often do as soon as I wake up. The strange end lingered and stayed very clear, being the part that woke me up. I stared out in the almost pitch-black room. Still early morning by the looks of it. I could hear Mike sleeping quietly. The abrupt end to my sleep left my mouth dry, and my head disorientated. I got out of bed and walked to the bathroom for some water.

I tiptoed by memory through the minefield of Mike's things scattered over the dark floor. I reached the bathroom door, surprised over, not stepping on a single item. I flicked on the lights, making me squint my eyes, waiting for them to adjust to the bright light as I walked to the sink. I flinched when I saw my reflection in the mirror.

The girl from my dream gawked back at me, wearing a short dark blue t-shirt and white bikini briefs with small red hearts dotted all over.

Is this still the dream? It can't be… I touched the glass, then ran my fingers through the long black hair, held a lock up against my nose.

That same scent. I touched my face, such smooth skin and soft lips…

No, this was real, however impossible it seemed. I looked at the two protruding bumps on the t-shirt; I gripped hold of the seam and pulled it up, gazing into the mirror. The same B cup sized teardrop breasts from the girl in my dream; I touched one with my hand while holding the cloth up with the other.

"Ooh yeah!" Surprisingly real and strange. I bent forward, looking down toward my crotch covered by the heart dotted panties. That was a woman's crotch, not a man's, not a shadow of a doubt. I moved my hand down and touched through the fabric, and for the first time, felt my very own pussy lips. An incredibly sensitive and new sensation passed through me to such a degree, I instantly redrew my hand. I looked again into the mirror, lost for words holding my breath.

"You're up early today." I twitched, letting out a squeal startled by hearing a girl's voice, by the bathroom door, while I was investigating my shocking new female shape.

"Sorry, didn't mean to scare you, Tina." I recognized the voice and looked toward the door opening. The girl with the auburn colored hair from the party last night was standing there wearing a black t-shirt and a pair of gray bikinis briefs.

"W-What are you doing here?"

I stuttered out of breath; my pulse racing even faster. My mind tried to grasp how and why she stood there. Had Mike brought her…? It wouldn't surprise me; nothing was safe from that hound dog. Still supporting myself against the sink, with my left hand, from the scare; I clawed my fingers into the edge; for a moment forgetting all about my girly looks, and the fact she called me Tina.

"What you mean silly, I live here." She looked puzzled at me. "I'm Natalie, remember?"

"Natalie?"

"Yeah, I switched college before my 3rd semester. I transferred here and became your roommate a few weeks ago, since you had none after yours switched too."

"I… I'm sorry, but..." My brain was now in total overload, not a single thing she said made any sense to me.

"Were you at the party too? I didn't see you there?"

"Uh yeah..."

"Then a bit of friendly advice, hun. You really shouldn't drink so much on a school night that you can't even remember your roommate the next morning." She giggled heartily and came over and hugged me. A wonderful delicate scent of jasmine reached my nose.

"I'll keep that in mind."

"Okay, my alarm goes off in 10 minutes, so no sense in trying to sleep more. Let me know when you're done out here." She left, flashing me a smile as she passed through the doorway.

I noticed for the first time this bathroom, while the same arrangement, it wasn't in any way my usual. Here were other shampoos, the bath curtain had another color, and there were several female related products. I turned on the cold water and splashed some into my face, trying to clear my mind.

I stared back at my reflection. Tina? She called me Tina. But how had I ended up being this gorgeous girl and roommates with Natalie, the girl from last night's party?

I took a deep breath and looked down over my now female body. My eyes caught the heart dotted briefs; if anyone had been standing beside me, they might have seen a huge light bulb switch on over my head. That mysterious goth hippie girl, the riddled question, and strange heart. Maybe she was some kind of modern witch? My logic minded brain insisted that no such thing exists. None the less, it was the only explanation I could think of at this time.

I rushed out of the bathroom. I needed to check the heart by the bed. The sun had begun to light up the room.

This was definitely not my old room at the boy's dorm; this was a completely different room. The size and setup were the same. Two beds, one on each side with two dressers between them where the window was. At the end of each bed were a small workspace and chair with room for a laptop or books. Natalie was sitting on the edge of her bed, swiping and tapping on her smartphone. So the bed on the left had to be mine, which was the same side as before.

"I'm done out there for now."

I looked for the heart, but it wasn't on the dresser. The only thing laying there was the room key and phone. It looked like my phone, but instead of a protective case with an illusion of bullet holes, it now had a red rose marbled case; quite stylish and girly looking.

"Okay, you feeling better again, hun?" She threw the phone light aside on her bed and looked at me.

"Yeah, thanks, I woke up from a strange dream which left me confused."

"Something you want to talk about?"

"Maybe another time."

"Okay." She got off the bed and, with feather-light steps, headed for the bathroom. Just before she vanished in behind the closed bathroom door, she pulled her t-shirt off and threw it on the chair.

I caught a glimpse of what looked like a perfectly shaped breast and what an ass she had. An unknown warmth awoke in my lower belly, to the sound of the shower running, and Natalie's velvety voice humming happily.

CHAPTER 3

A fact that, so far, had eluded me in my shaken… or shocking state would be more right, suddenly became obvious to me. What good was it to know her name and be her roommate when she'd turned me into a girl to achieve it? I mean, it wasn't a platonic friendship I sought.

Another scary thought made me clench my teeth. What if the witch had switched my personality with her roommate? Would she then be Tom now and living with Mike? I had to know; I checked the different drawers of my dresser. I found some jeans, a gray hoodie, put it on swiftly, and jumped into a pair of pink sneakers standing in the tiny hallway. Natalie was still humming in the shower. I left and locked the door quietly. Based on the look of the room and view from the window, I was still in the same building, just in the girl's wing. I rushed down the stairs, running over to the entrance of the boy's wing, where Mike and I had our room. I sensed my new breasts bouncing freely under the hoodie.

Shit! I forgot a bra. This is all so new and different. I walked the last bit, not wanting half the boy's dorm noticing. They already scanned any pretty girl, who entered their side. I knew Mike did, and to be honest, I'd done too but less obvious. I headed up to the second floor and found number 217, our room. I knocked, filled with anxiety about what I'd find. It was Mike that opened the door, with a familiar hangover hit stare which seemed to clear up as he got a better look at me.

"Can I talk with Tom, please?"

"You're the wrong place, sweetheart!"

"Pretty sure you got a Tom living here, he's your roommate."

"I don't have any roommate yet this semester. A new guy is transferring next week, but I don't know his name. Is that Tom guy your boyfriend?"

I ignored his question, still thinking about how this all fitted together.

"So you don't know any Tom, not from last semester, either?"

"Nope!"

"Okay, sorry, my bad, then I must have gotten the wrong address."

"No problem, I'm Mike by the way. If you're new here, I can show you the most important places on campus later if you want?"

"Thanks for the offer, but I need to find my friend."

I left and headed back to Natalie's and apparently my room. I don't recall at all walking back; so deeply caught up thinking. My old self had ceased to exist, and now I was Tina instead, but who's Tina…? I locked myself in, hearing the blow-dryer in the bathroom.

I went over to the dresser and picked up my phone covered in the red marbled case. I turned on the screen: Tina Anderson. My last name was the same… I scrolled through my contacts. Gone were most of my old friends, including Mike's number. Replaced with several new ones I didn't know, including Natalie's number. I found my parent's home number and my older brother's; they were the same as before, how odd. I tapped my brother's; I wanted to hear if his voice was the same. I wouldn't say anything, since how should I explain this to him.

"Hi, sis, what's up?" I almost dropped the phone hearing him call me sis.

It was my brother all right, the same I'd known all of my life.

"Hello..? you there?"

"Uh... sorry I must have tapped you by mistake in my contacts."

"Ahh okay, talk to you later then, have a nice day, sis!"

"You too."

I stared dumbstruck at the end call icon showing 19 seconds. He knew I was his sister now...? I noticed the picture frame standing at the back of my dresser. A family picture showing my mom, dad, brother, and the girl, who was me now. I was erased from existence, replaced with Tina. But I still remembered my old life as Tom. I had no relocation of my past life as her. How should I fit into this new setting? I clutched the frame between my hands, on the verge of bursting into tears...

Natalie came out with a towel wrapped around her, throwing her gray panties into an orange laundry basket standing next to a black one by the bathroom door. She walked over to her dresser, picked up a pair of blue and white striped bikini briefs. She cast the towel aside on the edge of her bed, standing all naked as she bent down to put them on, only a few feet from me, sitting on my bed opposite her. It was unbelievable how sexy she was; firm round perfect breasts, a good A cup that fitted her slender frame. She'd light tan skin, so smooth and gorgeous. I spotted she shaved below too, as she pulled her panties up, and looked to my side. I rolled my eyes back down at my picture, ashamed she'd caught me ogling her.

"What's the matter, you suddenly become shy, huh?" She retorted with a smirk as she found a bra and started putting it on.

"Uh… no, I was far away in my thoughts and didn't want you to think I was staring at you."

"No worry, hun. I got nothing you haven't seen before or have yourself."

She laughed warmly and walked out to the bathroom again with her towel. It was a relief she took it so easy, and while she was right; I wasn't used to the so-called things I'd too, making a glance down at my chest. The breasts heaved under the hoodie with every breath making me think about the missing cock between my legs now replaced with a female vagina.

She came back and started to dress for class.

"Why aren't you getting ready, have you forgotten we have early English literatur together today?" She walked up before me and made a little scene on the floor in an overplayed fashion that cracked me up.

"You're mistaken, Mr. Darcy… had you behaved in a more gentlemanlike manner..." I applauded while trying to stop laughing. It was so funny but still a hard reminder of my current situation. I'd no memory of us studying English litterateur together, even if I recognized the scene was from Pride and Prejudice.

"I got some personal stuff I really need to sort out today. Would you be a sweetie and take notes for me?" I was postponing the inevitable moment where she'd discover that I was a complete phony.

"Okay, hope you get it solved, then we see late afternoon again?"

"Hope so too and sure," I replied. She put on a half long loose burgundy colored blouse that matched her black leggings well and packed her bag.

"See you!" she left, making briefly pouted lips toward me and a smile. She was incredible in every way, beautiful beyond words, funny, and sweet. My heart melted when I saw her, heard her, smelled her. But I was a girl now, with no knowledge of my current past, feeling utterly lost.

Someone knocked on the door. I walked over to open it, and stood face to face with the person responsible for my transformation; the mysterious girl from the party.

"You!"

"Yes, me. I wanted to see how you're settling into your new life."

"Why have you done this to me?" I screamed out as she strolled in and shut the door.

"You wanted to meet your heart's desire. I offered that possibility, and you obviously took it." Running a few fingers quickly through my long black hair.

"You forgot to mention it involved turning me into a girl, changing my whole life!"

"It's the only way you'll ever stand a chance with her… a little secret: she's into girls."

"…into girls?" I repeated, left almost speechless by the information.

"Yes, she is! You now have one and a half-day or precisely until Saturday midnight to find out if you two can find love together."

"But how? I don't even remember this new life? She'll end up thinking I've lost my mind when I can't recall anything we have talked about or done together?"

"In a moment, you'll remember your current past too. All will be natural to you." She opened the door and looked at me with a dead serious glare.

"I suggest you make the most of my generous gift. Else rest assured, come Saturday midnight you'll find yourself back in your bed in your messy room with your friend Mike. Knowing exactly why you'll never stand a chance with her." Then she left and shut the door behind her.

What she'd told filled me with huge relief, I could return to my old life again; this was just a temporary experience. Try to find true love with Natalie. Sure, that sounded great, but then I'd have to stay a girl forever. That was honestly a high price to pay for love. Though, I couldn't deny my extreme attraction to her in every way. The short moment of seeing her naked flashed for my eyes again added a sense of emerging wetness in my crotch; such a good feeling. In all fairness, I was a super sexy girl now that matched her amazing beauty."

Who wouldn't want to experience that for a few days? Some naughty ideas of sexual self-exploring nature emerged in my head. I'd breasts, real breasts, and a pussy… a moist pussy. I had the whole room to myself until late afternoon. The amazing possibilities flooded into me, now where my worries and confusion had vanished. New things to explore. I locked the door, removed all my clothes right down to the bikini briefs. I removed the covers, laid down on my back, and got ready to investigate this new body of mine.

Then a powerful surge hit my mind. New memories flooded in, people, places, scents, and sounds. It was astounding, I remembered it all now, my life as Tina, good stuff, bad stuff.

My first real kiss with a girl. A blonde girl named Emily last year of high school shortly before graduation. I hadn't dared to show my fascination for girls to anyone. I probably wasn't 100 percent sure myself until that time. We were in her room, a Friday evening I slept over and it was pretty innocent. Us kissing and a little cuddling, touching each other's breasts.

For her, it was just curious experimenting, something she giggled about afterward. For me, it was a lot more, a full-blown recognition of my attraction to girls over boys. Discovering how much it turned me on. An awakening of deep arousal inside that no boy ever had been able to ignite. I squeezed my breasts, one hand on each playfully making my nipples erect from twirling them gently between two fingers. This wasn't new to me anymore; I knew that move worked for me; I'd done it several times before playing with myself, masturbating, making my shaved tight sex soaking wet from arousal.

"Mmm," I muttered to myself, recalling Alyssa, who I'd met the first year here. She wasn't shy or quiet about being a lesbian girl. She lived off campus alone, and after a party, we ended up in her room. She was a slender girl with heavy curves; short black hair with pink bangs. She was my first true sexual girl on girl experience and taught me a lot. I remembered how she fondled my breasts and touched my nipples the same way. Made them so hard and turned me on like crazy. I mimicked her touch from memory.

So good! I remembered how she kissed her way down my neck with tiny delicate wet touches. Her lips gently against the skin, moving slowly over my collarbone, so sensitive toward my breasts where she stuck out her tongue and licked her way onto my nipple. She let the wet soft tip circle it while she pushed the breast upward from below with her hand. Licks and touches that drove me wild and warm deep inside my crotch made me so wet. She flickered her wet tongue over the nipple harder while squeezing the other breast, making me moan out. Feeling her soft wet tongue work first one nipple, and then switch to the other, letting the cool air kiss the wetted nipple so refreshingly, it felt as stiffening even harder.

She worked her way down my stomach toward the place I wanted her to kiss tenderly, lick good and fuck deep. She kissed above my pubic bone as I bent my legs up, giving her the space she needed.

I shivered in pleasure as the full length of her tongue brushed all over my soaking wet sex. I arched my back while purring loud, letting her hear my pleasure.

She licked up my juices with her own satisfying sound, sending waves of joy through my every fiber. She centered on my clit, licking it rapidly, coaxing it from its hiding. It was the best feeling ever, her soft, constantly circling tongue that swept over it up and down, side to side. I moaned out louder; it was so amazing as her supple tongue moved toward my tight wet opening. She bent the tip into me, licking all the way around.

"Ohh. yes, yes!" I was getting so steamed up, starting to gasp for air. Every tiny touch she made echoed like thunder inside me, making me squirm on the bed. She soon replaced her tongue with something much firmer as she bent two fingers into me, rubbing against my walls. I recalled it so vibrantly, massaging my wet crotch with my hand and repeated her moves. I bent a couple of fingers into myself. It was almost not masturbating, but like her doing it to me all over again. I kept my eyes closed and the memory rolling while fingering myself the same way.

She fingered me deeper with soft, constant moves that caressed my insides; brought out a soft squishing sound of her fingers working my soaking depths. It sent tense emotions rocketing through me that made my juices flow.

"Ooh, yes… fuck, yes!" I cried out, writhing and trying to force my sex harder against her hand as she started massaging my clit with her thumb. She'd her fingers buried inside me, caressing so sensitive places. My climax neared, marched on by powerful sensations she caused inside me. I clenched around her fingers.

"Ooh… oooh!" I cried out. My body surrendered as she made me cum. I shook as several surging waves erupted out from deep within my pussy, sending me into ecstasy and pure joy.

Recalling it while fingerfucking myself had pushed me over my edge. I panted loud as the shivers centered out from my lower tummy. It moved all the way out through my legs to my feet. A warm explosion that also moved up through my body in pulsing waves of pure bliss.

My arched up back, dropped flat on the bed, still gasping loud. My heart raced beneath my heaving breasts, sweaty, and warm. This was such a perfect moment of satisfaction.

CHAPTER 4

The raging ocean that had stormed inside me calmed down as I laid and tried to compare memories of my previous life, and this of being Tina, compared sex. In all honesty, Tina's world was a good one. My parents and brother were the same, good friends, and the sex lacked nothing. It was different but so incredible good.

Alyssa and I were together several times that first year. It was strictly for the sex, exploring ourselves and satisfying our needs while having fun doing so. We were simply way too different for anything beyond that, also moving in different social circles. For that reason, we gradually slipped away from each other. Not that there was anything bad between us. We chatted friendly if we met by coincidence. Natalie and I, though, that could be good. It had a lot of promise, something worth aiming for, even worth staying a girl for. It was a strange thought to consider not returning, but if she fancied me too, then yes.

I ran through my memories of the few weeks she and I'd been roommates. She was perfect in so many ways, not just her stunning looks, but she was smart, kind, and genuinely fun. We got off well together, had already become friends. The information about her being into girls seemed to be something she had never shared. Something she'd been secretive about. I couldn't blame her. I didn't exactly run around with a sign in bold letters on my back, posting it to all I met either. Though, that would have to change. With limited time assigned, there wasn't room to waste any more if I was going to be serious about us.

I got up and changed the sheets after my pleasurable moment. Then I spend a good deal of my time getting a relaxing shower, putting on my daily light makeup, and deciding what clothes to wear. I wanted something that presented me the best way, not too dull, not too flashy, and defiantly not too provocative.

After trying on several pieces of clothes, I ended up with a sleeveless tight fit, all black top, and a knee-length soft pink skirt. Something that looked great on me while still being casual enough for a normal evening at home. A text arrived on my phone from her.

"Hope you got your issue solved?" followed by a sweet red heart and "Up for sharing a pizza?"

I texted her back. "Sounds yummy, and yes, thanks!" Using the same red heart emoji to end my text. I pondered how I should bring up the subject, and open the possibility of her and I found together in a closer way than friends and roommates. I guess knowing she was a lesbian, the easiest would be to tell her I was and hope she'd open up too. Maybe even see more than just a friend in me. It was a little nerve-racking to sit and wait for her to return; my entire faith was at stake.

We'd talked and shared a lot, but relationships we hadn't touched beyond we both were single at the moment. I scrolled and found such a cute group selfie of us on my phone, taken a week ago in the campus park. We looked so good together. I'd have to look for an opening to tell her tonight.

She arrived moments later with our pizza; I'd already found the two plates we stored for when we ate some takeaway here; it was often when we did an all-nighter here studying.

"You look much better."

She said as we'd sat down on each of our beds facing each other with a pizza slice on our plates.

"Yeah, I'm back to normal," my reply given the whole situation made me giggle out loud.

"What?"

"Nothing, just a little tired. How was English literature with Ms. Stewart?"

"She can analyze it so much to pieces that it seems she reads too much into the texts."

"That bad, huh?"

"Yeah, she even suggested we watch a movie relating to Jane Austen to discuss modern adaptions next time."

"Yawn, I don't feel motivated for watching another movie build over Pride and Prejudice. For me, the book itself and the older mini-series supply me with the images I need of Elizabeth Bennet."

One pizza slice vanished, then another and another until we'd two empty plates standing on the dressers.

When we first got started, our talk just flowed so naturally that we easily lost an hour or two. I enjoyed her company, thrived on every second we spent together. It was like a place in the sun to be in her proximity.

Our talk had come full circle; passing classes, friends, clothes, old stories from our past about our families, and now ended back at a Jane Austen related movie, which she briefly checked on her tablet. She used that as her laptop and had a loose keyboard acting as a screen protective lid.

If it wasn't for our interesting conversation, I took part in with profound focus. I'd get so turned on from just looking at her, seeing those lips I wanted to kiss and feel against mine. I gazed at her; that stunning body which I sensed the curves of through her clothes. I pictured her nude again, pieced together the small moments of her dressing or changing clothes, I'd seen the past weeks, into a hot collection, my very own peep show. I felt an added moisture below and a fuzzy warmth igniting inside my lower stomach, seeing the mental slideshow of her naked breasts and shaved sex pass through my mind.

"'Bridget Jones Diary' is here, that's based on a book inspired by Pride and Prejudice, hence the Mr. Darcy character. Wanná make it a movie night and watch it together? We can cuddle up on one of the beds."

"Sure," I replied. Cuddle, kiss, and much more! I could have screamed. It was a start, though I'd struggle to keep my loins in check.

Before long we were lying together on my bed. The tablet was resting against a pillow that lay across our stomachs. Two good friends together, that wonderful scent of her hair reached my nostrils again, the soft skin of her arm touching mine. Why should it also be so difficult to make that next move? I feared her reaction, worried she'd turn me down if I didn't get it right the first time.

I followed the movie or tried. It tormented my mind the limited time, the girl I loved... Yes, I loved her! I'd been with her enough to know she and I were meant for each other. Besides, I desired her, wanted to feel her naked body, those perky breasts pressed against mine, while we kiss and... I bit my lower lip hard. Thinking more thoughts like this would make my panties soaking wet and risk she senses it.

The movie ended, and I couldn't care less, but added.

"That should satisfy Ms. Stewart's wishes for modern thoughts on Jane Austen."

"Speaking of her, I think she's lesbian," she suddenly said and giggled.

"Lesbian? Jane Austen?"

"No, silly, Ms. Stewart."

"Ms. Stewart? why you think so?" I turned and almost gawked from sheer surprise.

"It was something she said today about the past few decades of debate regarding the author and the possibility of lesbians in her books. It seemed to matter a lot to her to point that out, more than usual. So I wondered if it were down to a thing she valued personally."

"Could be, it can be hard to judge just by appearance who are and who aren't."

She looked thoughtful; for a moment, I hoped she'd take the step and tell me about herself, but when that didn't seem to happen, I'd to.

"I have to tell you something."

"What?" She turned to her side toward me, resting her head on the arm.

"I'm lesbian… I have known it for the past year or two, probably also some years before. That something was different for me. It's not something I have been so open about, not sure why. Maybe I've just felt safer keeping it to myself, most of the time."

She gazed at me with her intense blue eyes as we faced each other with only a hand's length between her lips and mine. Her face was frozen in the same expression she'd while I told her. Was she surprised to learn, maybe even happy? Her silence probably only lasted some seconds, but each felt like minutes to me. I wanted to break the stalemate, and the only way I could think of was to let my emotions guide me. I leaned over and kissed her, felt those soft lips of my desires against mine. For a short moment, I sensed she kissed me back, making my heart skip a beat. She didn't move away but pressed them against mine.

Beep… Beep… Beep…!

An alarm went off. It was the phone over on her bed, making her twitch and break our far too short kiss. She rushed off the bed to go grab it.

"Sorry was by the shop today to get the faulty battery, I told you about replaced. It seems that reset my morning alarm to default midnight instead."

She turned it off.

"I'm glad you felt you could tell me… but uh... I'm sorry. It's been a long day, and it's getting late… Perhaps we can talk more about it tomorrow… Is it okay if I use the bathroom first tonight?"

"Sure."

She seemed beside herself, speaking incoherently.

I'd never seen her like this before as she vanished out there. I wanted to slam her phone against the wall. It stole our moment, and now she acted all weird.

Having her on my mind all evening, laying close, and finally kissing before it ended in nothing. I needed to cum feeling so horny. I pushed the window open to ventilate our room, grabbed my purple vibrator I hid in the bottom of my underwear drawer, and laid a towel on the bed. I pulled my skirt up and removed my panties. As expected, they already had a wet patch from my arousal. I knew I max had 15 minutes, but already worked up, that would be enough.

While hearing the shower in the bathroom, I bent my legs up, and rubbed my wet sex good and fast…

"Mmm, yes," my warm juices covered my hand. Just touching my sex sent a pleasing sensation through me. I needed this so badly, pressed my fingers against my lips, rubbing back and forth. Then I made room for, I with the vibrator in the other hand, could push the tip against my clit while running it on the low setting.

"Mmm… ahh so good." I kept it there, let the vibrations move through me like an electric current. Then I moved it and started to drill the vibrator slowly into my soaking depths. It eased in and pushed against my insides. So fucking good. I pressed it all the way in, making me feel so filled.

"Ooh!" I moaned out, trying to keep it toned down, just closing my eyes and enjoying it. The buzzing vibration emanated out from inside me, through my entire pubic area, it was so pleasing. I turned up the power I wished to bring myself over the edge fast. I moved it slightly in and out of my dripping wet opening. I clutched harder around it as the vibrations surged even further out, pleasuring my g-spot and bringing me to my climax. Accompanied by waves pulsing out through me, it made me cum. I pulled it out and laid flat, breathing heavily, taking in the full moment of pure pleasure running through me. I wished I could have enjoyed it longer. But while still shivering slightly, I'd to pull my skirt down to cover up the towel, toy, and my pleasured wet crotch as I heard the bathroom door.

"Cool and fresh, huh? You mind if I close it?"

"No, I just thought we needed to freshen up the room."

I got up hiding my toy in the wet towel while she closed the window and got ready for bed. With slightly wobbly feet, I walked out to the bathroom.

While I showered, I wondered why she'd reacted that way and now pretended as nothing had happened. As if we hadn't kissed or knew I was into girls. It was also her irresistible lips and my burning desires fault. I should have given her time to react to my revelation. But I didn't have time. I had less than 24 hours left, how could I wait any longer. I finished up and got my toy cleaned too. When I came out, she faced in toward her wall side all cuddled up under the covers doing all she could to avoid seeing or talking with me. I dressed for bed and switched off the lights.

"Good night, Natalie."

"Good night." I wished she'd say more. Perhaps I should…? No, it was best to give her time and hope for the best. It took me a while to fall asleep, fearing it was over before it began. And all because of a rushed thoughtless kiss.

CHAPTER 5

I woke up to bright sunshine coming from the window. She and I always switched off the alarm on weekends so we could sleep longer unless one of us had plans early.

I hadn't heard any alarm, and judging by the angle of the light, it was late morning. As soon as my eyes adjusted to the sharply lit up room, I looked over to her bed; it was empty. I listened for water running in the bathroom, nothing either. I sat up and looked around. The things on her dresser were still here together with other of her belongings. I breathed a sigh of relief. For a moment, I feared she'd packed and left while I slept.

I got up and did my usual morning routine of showering, hair and makeup, and some fresh clothes. I picked my dark blouse and jeans. I was just done when she returned.

"Good, you're up."

"Yeah, it took a while before I fell asleep, so slept in late today."

"Me too or the late falling asleep bit, but I woke up early and went out for a walk to think."

"If this is about what happened last night, I want to..."

"Shh, please, there's something I need to say to you first."

She came over, and we sat down on my bed. She looked at me concerned and seemed nervous, wringing her hands slowly.

"Okay, I listen."

I wished I could have said sorry for the kiss I hated to see her like this because of me. She took my hand and held it in hers, looking at me.

"What you told me last night caught me off guard. I didn't know you were and had discovered I am too. So I choked, and then you kissed me. It was too much. I needed time since you're my friend. I'm very sorry for my poor reaction. I ignored that you opened your heart and told me something deeply personal."

I couldn't hold back anymore.

"Sweetie, it's me who's sorry... I should have given you time to take in my words and respond instead of kiss you right after."

My eyes teared up, while hers looked watery too, I needed to tell her my true feelings.

"As long as we are honest with each other, I need to get this off my chest. I'm hopelessly in love with you. I know this probably sounds overwhelming too. All I ask is if you'll give me a chance, and think about if we maybe can take it a step further than just being friends. That's unless you find me annoying and ugly?" The last words made her giggle warmly.

"I don't, Tina, not at all!"

"That's a great start, then perhaps I may invite you out for lunch now as our first date?"

"You may." We hugged long, while the feelings of relief and joy wrestled inside me for the first place, feeling her head rest against mine.

We walked to a corner cafe close to the campus area, which had become a favorite place of ours to hang out. We both got a delicious organic chicken sandwich, which we liked. Talked just as we always did. I sensed she seemed happier and freer today, same as I did. She saw me as a potential girlfriend now. Something she clearly hadn't considered possible until last night. Then we went out shopping. Mostly just browsing and ended with the modern art exhibition we'd talked about a few days earlier. We talked, laughed, and had a great day together, enjoying each other's company.

After a light dinner, we were walking back home.

"Now, I know why you had such a glass-like stare when you saw me naked."

"Guilty," I giggled with a smirk. She leaned in and whispered with a warm breath into my ear.

"Perhaps, you should give me something to look at too when we get home." She let the tip of her sweet tongue brush gently over the edge of my earlobe and shortly nibbled it between her lips.

"Sure," I sighed delightedly. "You know how to turn me on, and I hope you'll follow my example then?"

"Mmm, I will." She whispered, still keeping her lips pressed against my ear.

We barely got inside before I realized how much she'd warmed up to the thought of seeing me naked.

We barely got out of our jackets and shoes before she instantly came over and wrapped her arms around my waist and kissed me. It was a sweet reminder of the kiss from last night, which I longed for, and this time nothing would interrupt it. Kissing her, I put my arms gently around her neck. Her perky tits pressed against mine. She had me so aroused it was like a flick of a switch. Her hands caressed my body, gripped the seam of my blouse and pulled it off me. I reluctantly let go of our kiss to let it pass my head. As soon as it was off, I removed her t-shirt too.

Her dimpled smile beamed at me with naughty eyes, and brows added, making her look so seductively tempting.

"I desire you so much, babe. I want you more than the air I breathe. I'd change my entire life for you!"

"I'm not going anywhere." She unhooked the front clasp of her bra and let it slide off her arms, leaving her perfect round breasts free before my eyes. I reciprocated and unclasped the back of mine. She bit her lower lip by the sight of me doing, and it filled me with a warm feeling, knowing she liked what she saw. Our lips found each other again kissing while pressing and rubbing our tits together. As her nipples brushed against mine, they made them erect. Our tongues met and twirled together, making me slightly moan into our kiss. Her nipples turned hard too. I loved the feeling of breasts against breasts. It was just one of the added pleasures of being together with another woman.

I unbuttoned her pants and pulled the zipper down, then slipped my hand inside. I wanted to touch her pussy, and I craved to know if her panties were as damp as mine was by now. I moved my fingers, touched her lips through the fabric, felt the heat emanating from her crotch. I ran a finger gently along her slit, pushing the panties against it

She shivered a little and sighed into our kiss as her moisture drenched the thin fabric. She opened my jeans and pushed them past my hip so they could slide slowly down my legs. We made a brief, forced break to remove our pants. She went over to my bed and sat down. I removed my bikini briefs at the same time, leaving me completely naked before her. She'd desire burning out of those blue eyes, scanning me with a lustful appetite.

She laid down, keeping eye contact with me all the time. She lifted herself by her feet to push her panties past the hip before laying down again. I grabbed the side of them and pulled them off her legs. She was the definition of perfect and sexy, Just lying there all naked with a naughty smirk, showing off her round breasts, slender body, and so desirable shaved, tight sex looking so moist already.

I ran my fingertips up her smooth, slender legs to her inner thigh and beyond to the sound of her subtle sighs until I rubbed over her lips.

"Mmm…," she purred while I brushed my fingers flat up and down over her a few times, felt her wet them. I moved one finger to my mouth and licked her salty sweetness of it. Then I straddled her and moved one of the other fingers down to her mouth.

She licked my finger clean like it was a piece of the sweetest candy. After I bent down and kissed her again while I touched her breasts, fondled them under my fingers. Squeezed them gently, so she squirmed on the bed while running her fingers through my hair. The scent of us heating up, getting wet together was an added turn-on.

I wanted to know what she wished and how I could pleasure my dream girl, this our first of hopefully many times to come.

"Any desires, babe?" I whispered.

"Think of a number." She smiled deviously, pressing her lips firmly together. I knew exactly what she'd in mind.

"69?"

"Bingo!" she replied with an exhaling whisper, making me release an approved sigh. Right now, I could only think of one thing being better of me eating her pussy. That was her doing the same to me.

I reversed my straddle, leaned forward on my knees, facing her enticing wet lips. She pushed a pillow up under her head to better be able to reach my sex. She bent her legs as I ran my fingers up the backside of her thigh while resting on my other arm. My breasts just brushed gently against her skin as I leaned down and pressed my mouth against her folds, kissing her sex. It was so good, and I sensed her body twitch as I did, hearing a soft moan coming from her. I stuck out my tongue and ran it full length over her slit, licking up her juices. Just doing that made me even wetter from pure arousal. Then her fingers touched my soaking wet pussy, caressed my lips. She rubbed slowly over before spreading them.

"Ooh yeah!" I let out as her wet tongue touched my clit, then flickered softly over it in rapid succession sending sensational waves speeding through me.

She spread her legs more, giving me better access; I found her clit and licked it carefully, swept the tip of my tongue over it from side to side and up and down.

"Ahh!" She moaned, letting me hear she enjoyed this moment just as much as I did. She became wetter, and I licked it up like the purest nectar. I ran my tongue from her clit to her wet, tight entrance, and back. I could barely focus when she added a little more tension and pace to her licks. She was eating me up, and it was so amazing. I started gasping for air as my heart raced in my chest.

My juices were flowing, and her nimble tongue rubbed me so perfectly. I shivered in pure pleasure every time her tongue passed my swollen clit. She writhed on the bed, too, echoing my moans. I wanted our first time together to be perfect. Cumming together would be just that. I eased off or added more tension, so we stayed aligned based on her reactions and sounds. She used a couple of fingers to keep me more spread while she sucked up my juices; licked me into ecstasy.

"Mmm, babe!" She was incredibly skilled. Knew exactly how to pleasure the delicate nerves that emanated out from my sex, moving around my wet opening and back to my clit.

"Ooh, yes, babe!" I cried. She was licking me toward my climax. I turned my full attention to her clit, circled it with the tip of my tongue swirling over and around it.

"Ahh, fuck yes!" she cried out while shivering harder. She continued rubbing her tongue against my clit until I felt a wet eruption inside powering out from my depths, surging through me as she made me cum.

"Ooh... Oooh, FUCK YES!"

"Oooh, yes... Ahh... Ahhh!" She moaned and started clenching repeatedly; she was cumming too. I shook heavily, still resting on my trembling knees, while my upper torso dropped down against her.

My head rested against one of her thighs while I felt her shiver strongly through her legs. We gasped for our breath; none of us able to speak.

It was so wonderful, and I hoped she felt the same way. I turned shortly after and faced her again.

"Wow, that was sooo good!" She bit her tongue playful.

"It was AMAZING!" I replied.

We kissed again; we were both still so aroused that we continued as a couple of charged up dynamos for almost two more hours. We took turns using my long purple vibrator to penetrate each other. The one who held it was in complete control until she made the other cum. She drilled it in and out of me, still switched off. Keeping me on the verge of cumming for minutes by easing off several times until she suddenly thrust it so deep into me that I arched up. Then she switched it on the high setting, keeping it there while she flicked a finger over my clit. That's how she managed to give me a double orgasm, which I hadn't tried before. Having her naked before my eyes, while she did, was also the biggest turn on ever. How could my arousal not hit its peak when she worked my sex?

After we cuddled and kissed in the shower; we simply couldn't keep our hands off each other. I loved to run my fingers through her hair; touch her firm breasts and smooth skin. Feel her sex under my hand when I moved it between her legs, loved when her lips kissed mine. Just as good, it was to sense her hands caress every part of me. Eventually, we ran each other tired and ended up laying together on her bed dressed for sleep time, just cuddling peacefully.

"You know how I feel about you, Natalie. I love you, but…"

"But?"

"Do you love me…?"

She gazed into my eyes in silence for a few seconds.

"You're sweet, funny, gorgeous, and so sexy..."

"But…?"

"Yes, your firm butt is great, too," she giggled. "Yes, I love you, deeply and with all of my heart." She leaned over and kissed my lips with sweet and loving affection.

Beep… Beep... Beep…!

The midnight alarm went off and made me startled rush up sitting, looking down over myself. Then on her afraid of losing it all. But nothing changed, I was still here, in the bed with her.

"What's wrong? It's just that stupid alarm. I completely forgot to change it today because of all the wonderful things that happened." She reached for her phone and turned it off, smiling a little confused at me over my frightened reaction. I looked back at her, beaming with happiness.

"Nothing is wrong; everything is perfect!" I laid down again and snuggled in close with her, while the last reminiscence of my previous life vanished from my mind like an unreal fantasy.

Transformed into a Hot Babe

CHAPTER 1

"Here you go, Martin." Ida handed me the paper, swiftly looking at me with her dark green eyes and usual cheerful smile.

"Looking forward to the concert tomorrow? It's been far too long since we did that."

"Yeah, it's going to be great," I replied and gazed at her as she walked back to her desk, further down the long row of desks in the spacious open office. She looked as irresistible as ever with her long, blonde hair. She wore a sweet navy blue blouse today. It was just so tight that I could enjoy the roundness of her B-cup size breasts and flat stomach. Her waist curved out to a slender hip covered by a black skirt that stopped before her knees and showed off her cute round buttocks. Her legs were covered in dark stockings, and she wore a pair of office style, black high heels. She was fashionable and incredibly hot. My cock pressed hard against my pants.

I almost lost track of time; I often did when I saw her and leaned forward to study the report she'd given me before anyone caught me staring at her. The usual dull lines of sale statistics and cost numbers filled the paper. For the past few years, I'd been a 'number crusher drone' among thousands of others working at DNA SCI Corp. The company had become one of the world's most valuable and successful corporations in record time.

They'd been the first to map the human genome in a new way completely, that gave them an overview of every DNA building block a human consisted of, and more significant the way the blocks interconnected. The discovery had made it possible for them to develop several cures and treatments for else terminal illnesses. The name always impressed strangers at parties and gatherings when they asked where I worked.

The truth was, though, that I was only an average employee among so many others there, reading through figures and statistics, nothing exciting or special. I pondered, it also fitted me, average was a word that labeled me better than anything else. I wasn't a large, wide-shouldered man with huge muscles, or dashing looking for that matter—only average Martin in my mid-twenties, who never stood out from the crowd.

There had been girls in my life, one-night stands, and a few more steady relationships which didn't last, but the past half-year I'd been stuck... stuck because I'd a major crush on Ida. A girl I couldn't have because she wasn't into men.

I recalled again the company staff party where the alcohol had given me the courage to finally invite her to dance, even if she always seemed like someone way out of my league. She'd accepted, but when I after the dance told her that I found her beautiful and hot, she'd interrupted me promptly.

"Thanks, but you aren't my type." I assumed back then it was my looks she had meant. Not long after the same night while I was sitting on my own, at a corner table. I was licking my wounds and drinking a beer after her rejection; she'd sat down next to me and laid her hand friendly on my shoulder and said.

"Sorry, Martin didn't mean to brush you off harshly. I do find you nice always at the office. It's just that I'm into girls, so it has nothing to do with you."

After that night, a friendship had emerged between us. We were both part of a small group from the fifth floor that occasionally met for an after-work drink or went out for some events together, like the concert we'd planned this Friday. I should have moved on and looked for a girl that actually was interested in men, but I still couldn't get her out of my mind, even if she were blissfully unaware of it. I hid my attraction, in fear that it'd spoil the friendship we'd now.

"Martin…? Martin!" The sound of my name brought me abruptly out of my daydream. I looked distracted up from the report. A woman was standing in front of my desk with a serious expression.

"Yes?"

"I'm from Human Resources; please come up to the eighth floor at three o'clock today for a meeting." She said, as thoughts immediately rushed through my head.

Had it something to do with my work, or had they caught me staring too often at Ida. I didn't dare to ask and let a casual "OK" leave my lips. She turned and left with quickly paced steps. I peeked at the wall clock at the end of the office: Quarter past one.

At the same moment, Ida passed my desk and, with a slight giggle remarked. "Already waiting for the workday to end?" I struggled to laugh, with her being concerned about the meeting.

I hope I'm not getting sacked. It'd be tough to find a similar job in this city, and the salary was decent. The worst was it'd spoil things with Ida. We could still meet outside of work, but I knew how the dynamics of a friend's group like this worked. I wouldn't be part of the lunch break chat, which was where someone would suggest a concert or movie. It was also where we agreed to meet after work to go to a club. Things I'd miss out on and slowly vanish from the group.

I rested my head covered in a cold sweat in my palms. It had happened that way with John after he quit a few months ago, and now it could be my turn.

"Ping!"

The sound of the elevator arriving on the eighth floor. I had only been here once, the day they hired me, and the place had its own reception right inside to receive applicants not used to the building.

A young woman with brown eyes and her dark blonde hair in a ponytail examined me quickly with a welcoming smile.

"You must be Martin; they're awaiting you. It's down the hallway second door on your left."

"Thanks." I smiled back and walked there, though deep inside, a cold chill ran down my spine. They? This sounds serious.

I knocked gently and entered a medium-sized meeting room. There was a wide oval-shaped modern wooden table in the middle and six designer chairs around it. The place had no windows, which made it appear somewhat confined, but it was well lit from the built-in ceiling lights. Inside, a woman probably in her late thirties got up from a chair. She looked like someone from Human Resources management, with her wine red colored matching jacket and skirt matched with an expensive-looking silk scarf. Her auburn hair was in a stylish bun like only women knew how to do.

"Welcome, Martin, good you could be here; I'm Marcy." She said in an over welcoming tone.

"Thank you." As if I had any choice, but it didn't sound as I'd done something wrong. I thought to myself.

I sat down opposite her and an older man looking to be in his fifties. He reminded me of a blend between a mad scientist and a nerd. He'd thin wild gray hair and a pair of squared thick glasses that matched the shape of his face. Several deep wrinkles filled his forehead and jaw. He was wearing a white lab coat from the research department. He hadn't said a word, and not even cared to look up from the notes before him.

"This is Dr. Larsson, one of our leading scientists involved in a promising project," She explained, making a slight hand gesture toward the gray-haired man.

For the first time since I arrived, he lifted his head and turned his gray-blue eyes at me with a piercing stare, like he was examining me. A gentle smile came over his dry lips.

"The reason you have been summoned is that our survey shows that you'd be ideal for our current breakthrough project." He said with a deep, rusty voice.

"Survey?"

"Yes, the two hundred question personnel test all applicants answer when hired here." He said eagerly. I hadn't thought about that after they employed me, but I recalled some of the questions made little sense. I'd presumed it was to psychological evaluate who would be skilled and socially adept employees. People that could perform effectively both individually and in teams as modern large working places required, but what did that have to do with a research project?

He stared directly at me and wrinkled his forehead.

"You were a hundred percent accurate in that test, correct?"

"Sure!" rushed out of my mouth. Honestly, I didn't recall it anymore. I always tried to be honest. If I'd been somewhat generous on some of my answers, where I sensed what they probably wanted, was long forgotten. I was fresh out of college, and this job was my opportunity for some real work experience for my resume.

"Terrific!" He chuckled with a grin, as Marcy took over.

"We'd like you to join the project and pay you ten thousand on top of your wage for your cooperation. Let me stress; this is a huge possibility for your future career here."

The amount rang in my head. I could replace my old unreliable car, but so far, they hadn't provided any information about what it involved.

"Thanks for the offer, but what is it you want me to do?"

Their faces turned serious again.

"For competitive reasons, it's a secret venture, that we see huge prospects in." He stretched his arms far out to each side as if he showed the size of a prize trout he'd caught.

"We have reached a point where we need a human test. You have been identified as the perfect subject, if I may put it so boldly."

He leaned forward at the table as his eyes opened wider.

"I can reveal it has to do with human improvement and change." She jumped in instantly his sentence ended. "We can't say more, but if you agree, you must sign this non-disclosure agreement. I think it'd be a mistake if you pass on this opportunity, Martin." Tapping her fingers on the red plastic folder lying in front of her.

Improvement and change? Were they going to increase my muscles or make me more handsome, or maybe even smarter? It sounded strange and a little scary, but I wouldn't mind becoming more than my boring plain self. Perhaps this was my opportunity to move up in the world.

"It's not dangerous to my health or something like that?"

He laughed.

"Not at all, a group of highly skilled scientists has worked on this for a considerable amount of time, and either it proceeds as expected, or nothing will happen. That we're confident about."

She pushed the folder with the contract and a pen toward me. It consisted of twenty closely written pages of legal mumbo-jumbo, impossible to find head or tail in for anyone but cooperate lawyers. On the last page was a line for my signature and specification of the ten thousand. They made it sound as I'd nothing to lose and only things to gain, so I signed it and handed it back to her.

"OK, what now?"

"Welcome to project Double-X, see you tomorrow morning at seven o'clock, building C, the main entrance." He grinned.

CHAPTER 2

The morning was chilly and clear as I parked near the specified building. It was a vast complex hidden behind the large office building where I worked.

I hadn't slept well; it had all rummaged in my brain.

What had I gotten myself into? Improvement, change, what was it from the personnel test that had made me such a fitting test subject? The money sounded great, though, and maybe even a forthcoming promotion insight.

I'd texted Ida before I left my apartment.

"Not coming to work today, top-secret mission." Her reply had arrived as I checked my phone while I walked across the parking lot toward the entrance.

"You're sure you aren't playing hooky?" Cute, if she just knew where I was, but I couldn't reveal anything.

A security check and two huge male guards awaited me inside, where they asked me to turn over my mobile and show ID.

A quick check on their screen cleared me. Then they told me to take a seat over by the waiting area past the control. I walked toward the three black wooden chairs surrounding a small cafe table. Most of the place was shiny white surfaces like taken out of a fancy sci-fi movie. After a few minutes, a girl looking around my age arrived wearing a lab coat similar to the one Dr. Larsson wore yesterday.

"Please follow me, Martin," she asked. I left my seat and accompanied her down a lengthy corridor. We passed a few doors in various sharp colors until we stopped at a bright red one with no markings. She ran her security card through the electronic wall panel and typed a few buttons. It unlocked, and she pushed it open.

"Please enter and take off all your clothes. There's a robe for you to wear inside, then someone will pick you up in a short while."

I stepped inside while the door closed and locked behind me. It was small and similar style white as outside, with a few lights along the ceiling edge. There was an identical red door on the opposite side. Against the wall stood a wooden bench in the same style as I'd encountered in a gym, on it laid a gray robe. On the wall toward the bench hung a narrow dressing mirror.

I removed my clothes fast and grabbed the robe, but before I put it on, I checked myself in the mirror.

Wonder if I'll become a chick magnet. I did a poorly, attempted, macho smile while making a few moves. I bend my arms as bodybuilders always seemed to do to flex their over-sized muscles. I put it on and tied it as the other door opened. Dr Larsson entered with a happy smile on his face.

"Good to see you again and ready too. Come with me."

The lab I entered was extensive, with several huge blue-tinted screens filled with figures and complicated looking data. Cables and tubes ran from tanks to instruments in an intricate grid all over the place. In the center of the room was what appeared to be an advanced medical bed with some straps attached, all sharply lit from above. It had a glass frame around it that raised from the floor to the edge of it. There were two large tubes connected to the frame. A few people, all in lab coats, tapping focused on the touch screens in the background.

"This is your spot," he pointed at the bed with one finger.

"Please remove your robe and lay down on your back. An assistant will prepare you for the procedure." I paused and, for a few seconds, switched my stare between the unusual contraption and the doctor, becoming unsure about the whole situation.

"According to your test, you shouldn't be shy either." He declared with deep laughter and walked toward a large control panel at the far end of the lab.

"Hmm," I mumbled almost silently as my mouth had gone dry. I wasn't shy, but not used to be exposed in such a spotlight either. I removed the robe and quickly jumped up and laid down. I rested my arms along my side while bending my elbows so I could cover my dick with my hands. How long should I lay here as a showpiece? At the same moment, a female assistant arrived. The bright light above turned the surroundings so dim I could scarcely see her, but her soft-toned voice sounded cute.

"You'll need to rest both your arms out along your body with your palms flat down toward the surface; else you can't fit inside." I removed my hands from my dick. Not like I'd anything to be embarrassed about regarding the size of my cock. I wanted to ask her what she meant with fit inside, but before my thoughts lingered further about it, she strapped first my arms and then my legs to the bed.

It was rather kinky, or it would have been if it didn't happen under this sharp light in a strange laboratory.

"Now you're all set. Remember to relax and breathe normally." She said and vanished into the shadows again.

Suddenly a loud machine hum started, and a shadow moved down from the ceiling. I hadn't noticed it when I arrived or after I laid down. The bright light had prevented me from seeing it until now where it came closer. It was a large kind of glass lid that fitted with the glass frame surrounding the bed. It closed down over me and encapsulated me with a heavy vacuum snap, as it shut tight. There were only a few inches of space to spare between it and my body on all sides.

A pinkish gas began to stream in. It clouded the glass, so the light barely passed through anymore and made it impossible to see anything. It tickled my skin as it surrounded me. I took a breath and inhaled the gas. It was odorless but a little warm and felt tender inside me. I didn't feel affected by it, even after several minutes of breathing it. As suddenly as it had begun, the gas vanished, and it cleared up. I squinted as the sharp light shone through the glass again. The noise of the lid moving up returned, and it disappeared up and out of my sight.

The same girl arrived again. I recognized her voice as she untied the straps. "See, that wasn't so bad, was it?"

I sat up and tried to study myself for any changes. I didn't seem different at all, though the light blinded me still.

"Am I done?" I asked, slightly confused.

"For now, you are. Let me help you with the robe and then follow me." She helped me into it quickly and took my arm. She led me to a door on the far side of the lab.

"You can rest here." I walked inside and heard the door lock behind me.

The room wasn't large. As my sight slowly improved, I could see it looked similar to the one I undressed in, but in this, the entire wall opposite the door was one large mirror. On the same side, as the entrance was a bed, the upper part was elevated, so the upper body and head would be angled upward when laying on it. As I glanced at the far end corner and focused on what was there, I felt warm, and the room spun, it came rapidly. I threw the robe aside and almost stumbled onto the bed and laid on my back. From the tilted position, I stared right at myself in the mirror. As I did, my vision turned black, and I passed out.

I woke up to a sharp shiver of coldness running through me.

What's happening to me? I looked scared. It was like my entire body fat vanished from my body within seconds, while my muscles were diminishing too. My skin couldn't adapt so fast and became baggy and wrinkled all over my now slim body and thin limbs. It looked several sizes too big for me. Then the skin started to tighten up.

In mere seconds it shrunk and became tight again but also completely hairless. To my horror, I saw the contours of my bones through it all over, like I'd never eaten a thing or ever moved a muscle. This was no improvement. I wanted to jump up and scream in pure panic, but I couldn't move a limb. I could scarcely even move my jaw to open my mouth, and no sound came from me.

What have they conned me into? Cold chills ran slowly through me deep inside. I was powerless laying there, my arms and legs unable to move at all. I didn't dare to check my face in the mirror. I dreaded far too much what I'd see. Suddenly the coldness vanished. It seemed as muscles and body fat started to return. It began down at my feet and legs. The nerves twitched. I looked more natural again, but my legs weren't manly at all.

They seemed more delicate and with feminine, smooth hairless skin and smaller muscles. My thighs looked the same as they reshaped. I saw a curve form on my outer thighs as a rapid pain moved through my hip. I raised slightly up as the fat returned under my ass. A curved waist shaped, and a slender toned stomach with a narrow vertical bellybutton formed. My arms didn't regain their old form either but looked thinner and female while my hands looked elegant with long nails. It tightened in my entire face and a minor pain shot through my jaw, nose, and cheekbone while my lips somehow felt swollen.

My strength finally returned in my limbs. I rushed my hands to my face and touched. It was so smooth, and the lines felt changed. My nose was smaller and fine, and my lips were softer and fuller. Something tickled my shoulders as I discovered dark brown wavy strands of hair grew down from my head. I pushed it aside and sat up straight and gazed into the mirror.

A beautiful face of a girl in her early twenties that could be a model stared at me with a shocked expression. Perfect cheekbones and nose, full lips, and big blue eyes, all framed in perfect thick, long shiny brown hair. I gawked down over myself.

"What's this!" I screamed out loud, but the voice I heard wasn't my own, it was much softer and high toned. I looked like a slender female, but while my upper body seemed narrower too than it used to be, there were no breasts, and between my now girly looking thighs, I saw my cock.

What had they done to me…? "Improvement, my ass!" I groaned, but as I did, a strange sensation hammered in my chest. I dropped back as my nipples became larger, and breasts grew out of my chest, slowly expanding larger. I moaned faintly as I saw a perfect pair of large, teardrop-shaped breasts with pink nipples. I'd to touch them, so soft skin, so sensitive, especially the nipples, were a lot more sensitive than I ever imagined women's nipples. I sighed as my fingers caressed them some more. My cock hardened massively. Groping my new bosom and now stiffened nipples was a tremendous turn on.

Suddenly, the feeling from my dick changed and vanished completely. I immediately sat up to look at it. My before so stiff dick lay long and flat between my thighs like a stretched out used condom, an empty hollow piece of skin. It was a shocking sight, and I instantly wanted to grab my now so poorly looking manhood, but starting from the tip, it began to invert into itself and vanish slowly.

It was as something entered me between my legs. I'd never felt anything like that before. It was a mix of slight pain and something quite arousing that made me quiver. When I checked again, my dick was gone. All I saw was a small entrance into me. My balls had vanished too, leaving only a wrinkled skin pouch that tightened up from both sides of my new entrance, until it concealed it and turned into smooth hairless pussy folds.

I jumped to my feet and gaped into the mirror. Before me stood a sight of perfection. My height appeared to be the same as before. At five foot nine, I was a below-average height man, but as a woman, I was a long-legged model. Beautiful breasts that bounced delightfully as I turned before the mirror to reveal a firm ass, not too big but with a perfect round curve from my back and down over it. I turned again, examining myself. Between my thighs, I now had what looked like a silky smooth female sex. I looked as I could have stepped right out of the bikini pages of a magazine, smoking hot from top to toe. Even without makeup, my face was stunning; I'd naturally long eyelashes, sweet pink lips, and to die for cheekbones.

I sat down, relieved on the bed. I'd survived this ordeal and hadn't ended up with four arms or legs, but this wasn't what I'd expected. This had to be a mistake or mix up; else, they hadn't been sincere.

What kind of experiment is it to turn a guy into a girl? I stared at my reflection again and got turned on by the hot naked stranger that stared back at me with an adorable pout look on her face. I laid down and closed my eyes as I let my hand wander down over my flat tummy and toward my pussy. I'd an immense urge to touch it, feel it beneath my fingertips. I moaned gently as I rubbed the soft skin folds.

They felt real as my fingertips sent a wave of joy through me that made me wet there but also wanting more. I moved between my lips and found my clit and began to stroke it.

"Oh!" I moaned such extraordinary pleasure, letting my finger caress the little bud even more. I gripped and played with my new breasts with my free hand; such a thrill of feelings that rapidly shot through me from my lower body. This varied remarkably from when I'd masturbated as a man.

I became soaking wet as I stiffened through my body and arched my back resting on the top of my shoulders as I moaned again. My fingers moved faster with ease, lubricated in my own moisture, circling my now raised clit. The feelings grew tenser. In my new female form with so many new senses, I was about to cum the first time even without any penetration. I pinched my hardened nipple a little, rubbed it between my fingers as sensational shivers rushed through my body, filling me with warmth. I rubbed my clit intensely and felt my climax arriving as I made myself cum in a loud moan.

"Ooh!" I became wet on my inner thigh as I shuddered in several waves of after shaking before falling back flat. I breathed heavy, and my heart pounded in my chest. I closed my eyes, attempting to comprehend how I'd just experienced one of my most incredible sexual encounters ever. It was more than my brain could handle. My thoughts vanished, and my mind went blank.

CHAPTER 3

When I came to my senses again after I had made myself cum so pleasurable, I suddenly wondered about that large mirror.

Hopefully, it wasn't a double way mirror. The thought hadn't crossed my mind until this moment, but it wouldn't surprise me if the doctor, and who knows how many others, had followed my transformation, and self-pleasure moment from the other side.

The notion made me uncomfortable. I was extremely under-dressed, lying all naked. I studied the right side of the room and spotted a table and chair with some clothes lying on it. It was what I, in vain, had tried to focus on when the change had begun.

I picked up the robe from the floor and used it to clean myself quickly. Then I dug through the pile of clothes. The only underwear I could find was a purple black lacy bra and thong pantie both in soft fabric. They seemed a little skimpy but better than staying naked. I put on the pantie and strapped on the bra as I'd seen my previous relationships do in the morning.

As I examined what else I'd to choose between wearing, I heard the lock, and the door opened behind me.

In walked Dr. Larsson with a smirk.

"You're up and about already, I see, that's marvelous." He grinned while he gazed all over me.

"You call this marvelous?" My voice even higher pitched as I was furious.

"Was this your plan or a mistake?"

"Calm down, calm down. I'll explain in a moment, but I'll allow you some more time to get fully dressed. You can come outside afterward." He replied and left before I could think of more to say.

I turned again to the clothes. It was all women's clothing. Three different style dresses, a couple of blouses and skirts, this was obviously no mistake. My mind was thinking more clearly. I took a long-sleeved black dress in a soft, stretchy fabric and pulled it over my head and down over my body. It fitted me well but was tight and showed off my slender hourglass curves. It had a rounded neck cut that barely hid the purple bra. It was so short it stopped only halfway down my thighs. I put on a pair of narrow heeled, black velvety half-long boots that stood on the floor and zipped them up.

There were several products on the table which appeared to be various makeup articles. Honestly, I wouldn't know where to begin or how. Besides, I clearly had natural good looks, so that would be fine for now. I took one last glance at my reflection, tossed my long hair behind the shoulders, and left the room.

The lab was empty and dark except a few lights where I came out. Marcy had joined him, wearing the same outfit as yesterday just in another color and a different scarf, which was obviously her office attire.

"Let's go over here, we have a modest meeting room, where we can talk," he pointed toward a door not far away.

"Perhaps I can finally get some answers then." I hissed while followed them. My walk seemed peculiar, and it reminded me of something Ida once had told me. 'Women walk more with their hip than men do.' That and the case I wasn't used to high heels on my footwear, even if these boots weren't exactly stilettos, made my steps sort of clumsy. I decided to let my hip help, and it seemed more right with this body.

The meeting room had two lounge chairs and a matching couch in blue. Marcy seated herself on the sofa. I took a seat in one of the chairs, while he sat down in the other facing toward me. I swung my leg over the other; if they'd watched me from behind the mirror, I wasn't in the mood to show more today.

I crossed my arms under my breasts and with as firm a tone as I was able to with my new voice asked.

"Was turning me into a woman the plan all the time?"

They glanced at each other before he replied: "Yes, that's what project Double-X is all about, the two X's stand for the female sex chromosomes." He talked as if he was telling me something ordinary, like what he'd for dinner or how the weather was. I couldn't believe my ears.

"Why wasn't I told…? Why me…? C...Can you turn me back into myself?" I wailed as the questions flooded out of me.

He frowned and looked serious as he leaned forward.

"In part, you were informed that it involved improvement and change. Besides that, the contract you signed contained the information, even though I'll admit it was in legal terms, which can be difficult to understand." He looked a little sympathetic at me. "Regarding why you, that's simply based on your test. You were the best-fitting candidate on all perimeters for this, with questions thirty-two and ninety-seven in mind. I genuinely believe you'll see that too when this initial shock of the transformation has passed." He leaned back in the chair. "Besides, you have no living close family members, or in any current relationship, we checked."

"That's bullshit, and what were those questions about?" I cried in a mix of anger and confusion, since why should those be so crucial to single out.

"Thirty-two was: Do you have a feminine side? To which you answered: Yes. Ninety-seven was: Have you ever wanted to feel how it is to be a woman? Where you also answered: Yes." He stated.

My world came crashing down over me as I recalled the questions. The first I'd answered 'Yes' since I presumed that was what they wanted to hear. I always kept my desk and stuff tidy, tried to be friendly and helpful toward all around me and wasn't the loud type. Things often perceived as more feminine than masculine. Ninety-seven I remembered clearly now. I'd been close to answering it 'No' but had thought about how I after sex sometimes had wondered how it'd felt for her. I'd ended with marking the 'Yes' and proceeded to the next question.

How was I to know they'd take that so literally? I quivered and clenched my fists so tightly my long nails pressed painfully into my palms. I wanted to shout at them, but instead, my throat closed up tight, and I started to cry, something I hadn't done in my adult years.

This wasn't happening to me! Marcy came over and tried to soothe me while stroking me gently over my back.

"You need to understand this is a complete transformation. Your body does now, to a considerably higher degree, produce the female hormone estrogen, which also imparts your emotions and feelings different than what you have been used to," he explained. I managed to form a few words while the tears ran down my cheeks.

"Can… can you change me back, or is this for…" My voice snapped over; I could barely say it, "forever?"

The time before he answered seemed like an eternity.

"We don't have any reversal ability, so you should expect this transformation to be permanent, also considering we don't think a human body can endure such an extreme measure more than once.

I was sitting in the twilight in my old car at the parking lot, in a long black coat with a chic faux fur collar they'd provided me, together with the new clothes I was wearing. The rest of my time in building C had passed in a haze after the words about I'd be a female forever. Apparently, my name was now Martina. They'd altered all my papers through their extensive resources and contacts, also at the government. They had also sacked Martin, and employed Martina with a start the Monday after next week, in a comparable job just on another floor.

They even had so much control over their design of me, that they in advance had created an image of me for my new driver's license. It looked photo-real and was spot on as I compared it with the pretty stranger who stared at me in the rear-view mirror.

They'd done a comprehensive medical examination and psychological analysis, which they cleared as being satisfactory. Every month for the next year, I had to come for more similar tests for their research. They'd also reminded me that the penalty would be severe if I broke my non-disclosure agreement.

Else, I was free to do what I wanted with my new life, including leaving them for other employers, even if they hoped I'd continue to work there.

My payment was already in my account, they'd stated, though the money mattered very little right now. I stared emptily out at the purple sky above the shadowy buildings.

I'd no idea how to be a woman, and what about my sexuality, was I into men and big cocks too…? The thought alone made me squirm. It seemed I wasn't. They'd explained they didn't know how this would impact my mind.

I thought about Ida, now this had, in a considerably different way, ended exactly as I feared when I headed for the meeting yesterday. I lost my job on the fifth floor, never to see her cute face and hot body walking past my desk anymore…

The mental picture of her caused a warm pleasure inside me and especially in my crotch, even sensing some added moisture there. Women and Ida, in particular, still attracted me that was beyond doubt.

I was a lesbian girl… This was a fresh start for me with her. Now I was a female too, and a hot-looking one even, besides she already liked my personality before, it was just my gender that had been wrong.

The possibility excited me as I tightened my grip around the steering wheel, but how to do it… Meet her by a pretended coincidence, try to sweep her off her feet with my striking looks and charm, I glanced in the mirror and raised a brow at myself looking seductively.

But it'd still be a lie and pretense, and not how I preferred to do. I sighed heavily and pressed back against the seat. Mostly I wished to tell her all. Seek her aid in this situation where I more than ever needed someone who, for her whole life, knew how it was to be a female.

Surely I could entrust her with my secret. They'd undoubtedly fire her as a minimum if she told anyone, and she always cared for her friends. I pondered to myself and found my phone, "six o'clock" what a long awkward day…

Shit, it was Friday. Ever since that meeting yesterday I'd forgotten all about the concert we were attending at nine o'clock. Ida would surely be home getting ready for the evening. I couldn't phone her, she would never recognize my voice, and I preferred to tell her about this in person. She once said where she lived, but I had never been there.

I texted her. "Can I come by your place now, desperately need your help, Martin."

Gladly she texted me back a few minutes later.

"Sure, are you OK?" How should I respond to that? I couldn't so I started the car and drove to her place. It was gladly only fifteen minute's drive from here.

CHAPTER 4

I was standing at her apartment door, being so nervous as I rang the doorbell. She opened and stared out at me with a puzzled expression.

"Yes?"

"It's me, Martin, can I please come in? I asked with my now girly voice, hoping she'd believe me.

"Martin?" She studied me with a skeptical glance as she squinted and checked to both sides of the hallway, perhaps expecting to see herself a victim of a practical joke.

"I texted you a moment ago; it's really me." I whimpered, trying to convince her as she looked up and down of me a few more times with a wandering gaze.

"Come in. When you earlier today texted me about a secret mission, this wasn't in a million years what I expected." She said and let me in.

"Me either believe me," I muttered.

We sat down together on her white couch in the corner of her cozy living room. Her place was very girly and neat.

I told her about the meeting and how the experiment had turned me into the girl before her. She listened to my story with a disturbed expression. I felt relieved after I had told her all. I needed to share this crazy experience with someone. Gladly she believed me.

"That was some story, Martin or Martina; I probably should get used to calling you now… Can't believe they did this to you," she looked concerned. "Was the transformation complete, I mean… you know?" She nodded her head a few times down toward my crotch.

"From what they told me when they examined me, I should be as much a real female as you now." I shrugged and curled my legs up on the couch beside me.

She stared thoughtfully for a while and then broke the silence.

"Now that it has happened as it did, then be glad they turned you into such a stunningly beautiful girl. They definitely put a lot afford into that aspect." She smiled warmly and reassuring while she squeezed my hand softly. My heartbeat sped up as I blushed.

Suddenly she sat up straight.

"Do you still have the ticket for tonight?"

"It should be in my wallet in the coat's pocket."

"Great, what you say we take your new body out for a spin? You have talked about how much you looked forward to hearing that band for weeks." She suggested jumping off the couch.

"But I don't know how to be a girl, and all that follows with that," I muttered, falling back even harder against the couch cushions with a heavy sigh. I was incredibly insecure about heading out into the public, looking like this, meeting both coworkers and strangers.

She rested her hands on her hip, standing before me with pout lips.

"Martina, there's no sense in hiding, you'll need to get used to this, so it might as well be tonight. I'll be at your side all the time." Her verbal kick in my butt boosted my courage, and being together with her right now was the best thing imaginable.

You'll need some makeup, and I can lend you a purse that matches your dress. You can't run around with that man wallet of yours anymore." She walked into her bedroom and turned on the lights, waving me along with a quick wink of her hand.

Before long, she had added various makeup articles to the skin of my face before proceeding to my eyes, where she added a soft touch of eye shadow, some black eyeliner, and finished with my lashes.

"Just wait and see what difference this does, even to a face with natural beauty like yours." She said while working concentrated on adding a bit of blush to my cheekbones before finishing off with a glossy dark red lipstick.

"Done, expect to turn some heads tonight, hon." She looked satisfied with her efforts as she let me face the mirror at her makeup table.

My jaw dropped, I looked like I came fresh of the catwalk.

"You're a true artist," I said admiring my new femme fatale look.

Ida giggled sweetly, "perhaps, but it helps that your face is such a cute canvas." We laughed together; this was probably the best time I ever had with her.

Then she got her own makeup done and dressed for the evening. Showing no shyness in changing clothes with me around now where I'd become one of the girls too. Perhaps she assumed the change had made me be into men. The subject hadn't come up in our talk.

A fuzzy warmth grew inside my body as I gazed at her, fitting her breasts into a black push-up bra with a sweet lacy edge and pulled a matching black lacy pantie up over her shaved hairless pussy. Seeing her naked, after having fantasized about her so many times, was beyond words.

She looked even hotter naked in real life than I ever had imagined. Perfect perky round tits and a cute firm ass that matched. Her body wasn't toned but fit with a slender waist. Her two times a week, aerobics had paid dividends. I struggled not to show how turned on I was while I'd such an urge to caress my moist crotch.

She was gladly all too busy to notice; this was hardly the way either to let her know about my feelings for her. Time was running late as she swiftly put on a short neon orange dress that showed a bit of cleavage and a pair of dark brown mat leather boots.

Soon after, we were sitting together in the back of a cab heading to the concert, where we would meet the others. She'd lent me some gold-colored dangle clip-on earrings, which she said matched the chain shoulder-strap of the black purse she also had lent me. They didn't feel at all comfortable to my ears.

"Are these earrings supposed to squeeze my earlobes so bad."

"Yes, that's normal. You might as well learn that we girls often have to suffer a bit to look so stunning always." She giggled and leaned toward me.

"At least until you get your ears pierced, then it's more the weight of the earrings that's the issue…"

"Ears pierced…" I gasped, even though I, of course, knew women got that done. It had until now never been something I thought about. I must have looked startled since she moved closer.

"Just loosen up and enjoy your first night out as Martina and let me handle the others." She whispered reassuringly while she friendly rubbed her knee briefly against mine. Her touch sent a pleasurable shiver through me. I had to let her know that I still was so attracted to her, and find out if I had a chance with her. As soon as the right moment appeared, I'd do it.

"This is a good friend of mine, which I brought with the ticket I got from Martin since he couldn't come." She told my former coworker friends. No reason to cause too much talk about the sacking of the old me that they'd learn soon enough.

At first, I'd feared they somehow would recognize me, but my change from boring Martin to hot brunette Martina was so unlikely they didn't have a clue.

The concert went well, yet as great as the band was, I wasn't entirely able to distract from all the new and unusual feelings. Like my breasts bouncing slightly and heavy on my chest when I danced to the beat of the music. Or how my hip and legs moved differently, combined with being lighter than before with my delicate body. Afterward, we went to a nearby bar, we'd visited several times before.

"I'm good at guessing a girl's favorite cocktail." Julian, one of my now former coworkers, leaned over toward me.

"Hmm, you look like a margarita girl, tell me if I'm right and I'll get you one?" He looked at me with his most alluring smile tilting his head to the side. He was trying out his old girl scoring routine, which I'd seen him use several times before, but this time I found myself at the receiving end of it.

"You weren't even close, but thanks for the offer," I retorted. I didn't want to shoot him down hard but was far from interested in him thinking he would have any luck with me tonight.

Ida had been right about the head turns. I'd noticed the long gazes I'd gotten from guys and even girls both at the concert and here. Part of me was flattered. It was nice to be attractive, but part of me also felt like a piece of meat, scanned by horny men. Not long ago, I hadn't been much better myself, but now I understood how uncomfortable it could be for girls.

I'd also noticed she had looked at me differently than she ever had before. It was just a glance…, perhaps my mind was playing tricks on me, but it seemed like a glimpse of interest.

She ordered her usual orange looking cocktail with a piece of fruit on the rim of the glass and two straws which she loved to sip at. I bought the same tonight, typically else being a beer man before. It tasted very fruity sweet and girly, but I liked it. I was sipping at it while wondering if my taste buds had changed too. The atmosphere was festive, and the talk went about the music and old stories I'd heard before, but now had to pretend I hadn't until she suddenly grabbed my hand.

"Pardon us girls a moment. We need a brief trip to the ladies' room." I followed her out there. It was so unnatural to step into the women's restroom.

Inside it was much nicer than the men's one. There was a fresh perfume scent and a larger mirror and sink area. Gladly it was empty, so we'd it to ourselves.

"How are you holding up hon, all OK?"

"I'm doing fine, it's been really fun though from a much different perspective."

"I can imagine," she replied while nodding. "I noticed Julian tried his luck with you earlier in vain, seeing any other you fancy? With your smashing good looks, you could get anyone in the room tonight." She giggled and checked her hair and makeup in the mirror. This was my chance, as my pulse sped up.

"There is one…" I started with an anxious voice.

"Who?" she turned her eyes on me.

"It's you." I gazed straight into her beautiful green eyes. For a moment, she stared at me without saying a word, then she asked.

"So, the change didn't make you be into men?"

I stared down at the tiled floor and shook my head before looking up at her again.

"It's still you, I want." She said nothing, but her eyes sparkled as we neared each other slowly. Her lips met mine in a kiss. My hands embraced her and moved up her body while her tender fingers and palms caressed over me. Our breasts squeezed together; it was so phenomenal.

I forgot all about where we were until she broke the kiss and whispered.

"Let's continue this back at my place?" There was nothing I wanted more.

Fifteen minutes later, we'd said good night to the guys, and we were sitting in a cab, holding hands in silence as the dark city lit in the streetlights passed by us outside.

I'd an ache in my pussy. I couldn't wait for us to be at her apartment. I noticed she bit her lip, the thought of her turned on too made me a little wet in my crotch… This was so different and new to me, this warm arousal inside my body.

CHAPTER 5

As soon as we got inside the door, we virtually threw our purses, coats, and boots on the floor and started to kiss and caress each other again. Her lips were precisely as soft as they always had appeared and even better against my own full lips.

"I'm so turned on," I mumbled.

"I know how to help with that." She gasped and grabbed my hand.

She pulled me into the bedroom and over toward her queen-sized bed, with the soft-pink colored sheets. She pulled my black dress off me and threw it aside before pushing me gently down to sit on her bed. She removed her dress before my eyes, letting her breasts bounce free as she unclasped her bra. A sense of pleasure ran through me; she was so hot as I gaped on those firm tits of hers and her slender, sexy body.

"Well…?" She asked, with a crooked smile and glanced at my boobs, still partially covered by my purple and black bra, and then back at me with a lifted eyebrow.

I smiled. "Just amazed by how stunningly sexy you look." Then I took off my bra and let my breasts hang free. I scooted back on the bed and moved my arms behind me, so I leaned on my palms, shooting my chest forward, and looked back at her with a seductive gaze.

"So…?"

"Girl, you are truly a work of perfection." She purred with a mischievous expression. In a swift motion, she pushed her pantie down her legs and off, standing all naked as she leaned forward with a knee on the edge of the bed.

"I never have… you know… been together, girl/girl…" I sighed out, as an uncertainty came over me all of a sudden, on how to have sex with her without my cock.

"Shh!" she whispered as she moved up beside me on her knees and put a finger tenderly on my mouth.

"I know this is a whole new world for you, so let me be your guide tonight." She laid her hand flat on my chest, just above my breasts, and pushed me gently down onto my back. Then let it slide down between them, over my stomach, and onto the seam of my pantie. Her touch on my smooth skin was so enjoyable.

Then she pulled them off me, feeling the fabric sliding over my silky folds and off my legs.

"Mmm." I purred while I ran my fingers through my long wavy hair, almost unable to resist the wet ache between my legs. I let my thighs rub softly together to please the itch as I squirmed.

"Bend your legs a bit." She said, as she spread them slowly and pushed them up toward me in a slight bend position which let her have full access to my wet pussy. She crawled between my legs, looking into my eyes with a lustful glance as her fingers brushed over my sensitive folds and began caressing them.

It was much better than when I'd pleased myself earlier. Now it was the girl of my dreams all naked before me that touched me. I became extremely wet, and a warm thrill rushed through me inside.

"That's a real pussy, all right." She made a naughty smile and then leaned down and started to lick the soft flesh. It was like nothing I ever had felt before; it was incredible.

"Oh!"

"You like this?" She breathed between her licking.

"Oh, yes!" I moaned. She let her soft wet tongue find my clit and started to flicker over it in rapid succession. My wetness mixed with the moisture of her licks. I trembled and shook every time her tongue touched my sensitive clit. I clawed my fingers into the sheets, as her tongue moved in wider circles, licking my entire pussy, while she let out satisfying moans of her own.

My back arched up as I moaned again… No wonder girls always wanted this. I never knew pussy licks were so awesomely good. It was a lot more intense than any blowjobs had been.

My heavy breasts jiggled with every tremble. I gripped them and groped them smoothly. As my fingers caressed over my nipples, they turned stiff. Together with her licks, the feeling was unbelievable, as a warm, rushing tension moved throughout my body, all sweaty and moist.

It was my climax, and it happened rapidly. My heart hammered as she concentrated her licks again on my clit, letting her tongue stroke it fast and repeatedly. My sight blurred, and I saw bright white flashes for my eyes, as she made me cum. My body stiffened and shivered hard. Electric waves of pleasure surged through every nerve. I let out several high moans that resounded through the room. Then I sank flat on my back while the after shaking passed through me.

She was sitting on her knees, licking her lips.

"So, you enjoyed that?" She grinned.

"You're amazing and must be deaf if you didn't notice I did."

She giggled sweetly. "I have a bit of experience, but now where you have felt how incredible it is, I'm sure you could do the same." She moved up beside me and snuggled in close. She gazed at me with glowing eyes while letting a finger drift slowly over my breasts.

"You know…" She started with a seductive tone to her voice as her fingers touched my nipple. "It can be very diverse from girl to girl and from time to time, how quickly you can cum again. How do you feel right now?" She squinted as she moved her fingers from my nipple and onto her breast, that laid close in against me and touched it gently.

Feeling her touch, and then starring on her touching herself, had me turned on. It astonished me that was possible after the experience I just had.

"I'm pretty aroused still from all these new powerful emotions and with such a hot naked girl here beside me," I said.

"Good, then you'll enjoy another round. I wouldn't mind getting in on some too. You have really made me wet." She almost purred while her hand briefly rubbed her sex. She opened her mouth a bit and closed her eyes with a satisfied expression.

"You want me to do something for you?" I asked.

She opened her eyes again and looked straight at me with a naughty smirk.

"Oh, what I have in mind will please us both."

I touched the soft flesh of her breast gently. She purred again softly.

"What is it?" I asked while getting that warm sensation in my lower stomach again.

"Have you ever wondered how two pussies rubbing together feels?" She grinned as I smiled back at her.

Honestly, I hadn't, but now where I had one myself and sensed some of the most intense sexual emotions I ever tried, I couldn't wait to experience that too.

She positioned us diagonally on her bed for space and helped me move my legs into a scissor orientation with hers one over and another under mine. Just to have her smooth pussy so close to mine while her soft thighs slid against mine turned me on immensely. Seeing her slender body and firm tits jiggle move before me while she concentrated on helping me into the right laying position was an added perk. I leaned to the side as she pushed herself closer slowly.

"Just keep that position and let me do the last bit, it can be a little tricky if you haven't done before," she sighed. Her nipples appeared rock hard, and her velvety folds had gotten a wet shine to them. It added to my wetness, knowing it turned her on and made her wet together with me. It made it all the better.

My head swayed back a bit as I closed my eyes. Then I felt her wet pussy touched mine. She rubbed it slowly against so warm and incredible a moan burst out of me, just as I heard her do the same…

"Oh…! Oh, fuck!" I moaned as our juices mixed and made our crotches so slippery and wet. She gently added a bit more pressure. Our tender flesh rubbed together, sending intense pleasure bursts through me.

I pressed my thighs a little harder against hers, letting our soft skin push and move together. I opened my eyes and glanced over at Ida, her eyes closed, and mouth open, looking just as pleased as myself, while she made slight moans at every move she made. Her body was as damp as my own.

"More!" I panted.

"Oh, yeah!" She moaned as she moved a little quicker. I wasn't sure if it was parts of my pussy or parts of hers that pressed against my clit, but it brushed me so immensely good. It was heating me up as another climax was coming.

I started to shake as an explosion inside me flashed through every fiber of my being. I let out a series of loud moans and shook against her. She shivered and moaned loud too. I dropped onto my back as we slid apart while waves of shiver moved through me. She breathed heavily too as I got a glimpse of her lying on her back.

"You made me cum again," I whispered as I tried to catch my breath.

"Me too." She sighed.

A moment later, she crawled up close. I cuddled toward her and looked into her eyes. There was a glimmer there I hadn't seen before as she gazed at me.

"This was incredible… You are incredible, Ida!" I giggled, as her beautiful smile widened.

"So are you." She grinned. "I can show you a thing or two more, but that we save for next time."

"Next time?" I asked.

"Yeah, next time." She replied with a tired smile as she closed her eyes, rolled onto her side and snuggled even closer against me. I closed my eyes. All the new incredible experiences and a sense of pure happiness I hadn't felt before filled my mind as I laid here together with my dream girl. This transformation had turned out to be the best thing that ever had happened to me.

ABOUT THE AUTHOR

Thank you for reading my book. I hope you enjoyed the story. Please consider rating it or making a review on Amazon or Goodreads.

I have a soft spot for gender swap stories and have written these since my adult teen years, mostly to my own amusement, but also because I love to write. Now I have taken the leap and begun publishing my stories with the aim of entertain, arouse, and maybe scratch an itch with my stories mixing the erotic and romantic.

If you want to stay up-to-date on when I publish new books, you can follow me on Twitter @DanielaRLovejoy, and visit my website: www.danielarlovejoy.com

I'm also always happy to hear from my readers and can be contacted through my website.

XOXO
Daniela R. Lovejoy

OTHER PAPERBACKS
BY
DANIELA R. LOVEJOY

The Girls Club – The Complete Series

www.ingramcontent.com/pod-product-compliance
Lightning Source LLC
Chambersburg PA
CBHW072055150726
47999CB00005B/1791